USA TODAY BESTSELLING AUTHOR
NANCY WARREN

A BUNDT INSTRUMENT

THE GREAT WITCHES BAKING SHOW
BOOK 4

INTRODUCTION

A cozy English village, a baking contest...and Murder!

I can remember a time when I baked for fun. I loved dreaming up new recipes, trying different combinations of flavors. Sharing my creations with friends and family.

Now? I have nightmares where the TV cameras are on me and I'm baking naked. Or I open my oven and my cake pans are empty. You don't need to be Freud to figure out I'm freaking out. This week on The Great British Baking Contest could be my last. I am one bad bake away from being waved good-bye.

Sure, I'd get my weekends back, but I'd lose the excitement of being part of a popular reality show, of spending time with the other bakers who've become my friends, and, most important, of having time to snoop around Broomewode Hall for secrets about my origins.

When a heated argument breaks out in Broomewode village pub, I put it down to nerves. Until someone winds up dead.

How am I supposed to concentrate on European Bakes when I'm in the middle of a murder investigation?

With witches, ghosts, an energy vortex, a black cat and an ancient manor house that holds its secrets tight, this isn't your typical English village.

Taste this culinary cozy mystery series from USA Today Bestselling author Nancy Warren. Each book is a stand-alone mystery, though the books are linked. They offer good, clean fun, and, naturally, recipes.

"Fantastic series full of loveable characters."

The best way to keep up with new releases and special offers is to join Nancy's newsletter at **nancywarren.net**.

A BUNDT INSTRUMENT

CHAPTER 1

"Ta-da!" my voice rang out as I presented my latest baking marvel to Mildred. She floated closer, her white pinafore flapping in the gentle breeze that came through the open kitchen window. "What do you think?" I asked, feeling pretty pleased with myself.

Mildred's brow furrowed, and her nose crinkled with a look of distaste I'd come to recognize—and fear.

"Yer cake has a great hole in its center," she said, sounding as horrified as if Gateau were placing a dead mouse at her feet. "My mistress would have turned me out of the house without so much as a character reference if I'd ever dared serve her such a thing."

I sighed and shook my head. No matter how many times I explained modern living to Mildred, she couldn't get her head out of the Victorian times. My kitchen ghost had been the cook here in my cottage over a hundred and fifty years ago, and she was always critical of my efforts. *Dead or not, get with the times,* I wanted to say, but Mildred was a kind soul (in her own crotchety way), and I didn't want to upset her.

Of course, in her day, losing her job was her greatest fear. Mine, in the days of TV reality shows, was being humiliated in front of the millions of viewers who'd be watching me fail if I got sent home this week. As we entered week four of *The Great British Baking Contest,* I was practicing day and night, trying to up my game. I couldn't afford any screw-ups after my performance last week. I owed it to myself and to contest judge Elspeth Peach—who I now privately considered to be my witchy godmother.

"It's called a Bundt cake," I told Mildred. "It's supposed to look like that."

"Hmph. A Blunder cake more like." She chortled at her own joke.

Gateau, my black cat and familiar, was curled up on a chair beside the stove, watching us both. I'm sure if I could read cat-mind, Gateau would be despairing of my puny human efforts to bake the perfect cake. *Chill out,* she'd be thinking. *Go roll around in the sun.* She'd spent most of the morning in the garden already, chasing butterflies and having a good old scratch on the cobblestoned path. She couldn't get enough of rolling around on her belly. It was mid-May now, and I would have been outside with her, tending my herbs and enjoying the gloriously warm spring weather, if I hadn't been in such a panic about my baking. Instead, I'd spent the morning "embellishing" my white cotton tank top with splatters of vanilla extract and batter. Thank goodness there were no bonus points for being a tidy cook. The kitchen was a bomb site.

I was hanging on by a thread, and I knew it. I was one "blunder cake" away from saying goodbye to my new friends on the baking show and to my best chance of finding out the secrets of my parentage at Broomewode Hall.

I could not let that happen.

I stuck a fork in my cake, which made Mildred even more sour-faced. "I wish you could taste it, too," I told her. "I could use a second opinion."

She shook her head at me. "Why don't you try again, this time without the hole?" She floated away, back to whatever pressing ghostly business she had that us mere mortals weren't privy to.

I bit into the morsel of cake. Without a second set of taste buds around, I pretended to be a judge on the show. How would Jonathon Pine react? It seemed that he usually waited to see what Elspeth Peach would say and then weighed in with his opinion. I tried to taste the flavors and feel the texture critically as I chewed. When I'd swallowed, I put on a British accent and imitated celebrity judge Elspeth Peach. "Very good crumb on this cake, Poppy. The raspberry and lemon flavors are coming through nicely. But I feel you could do better."

Argh, even in my fantasies, Elspeth was critical. She was also right. I had to do better.

I looked around my kitchen for inspiration. It was my favorite room in this old cottage and the reason I'd bought it, even if it did come with Mildred, who was full of baking opinions and no help with the mortgage. The shelves were already bursting with baking ingredients: ground almonds, polenta, icing sugar, demerara sugar—every kind of flour under the sun. Rows of mason jars were filled with sour cherries, currants, desiccated coconut, colorful sprinkles. I tried to always keep a healthy stock of produce so that any flash of sudden inspiration could be fulfilled immediately—you never knew when a good idea might strike you. But today I was lacking va-va-voom. At least the cake wasn't as sunken as my spirits.

This week's theme was something called European Bakes, and our first challenge was to make a cake with a European history. After a ton of research (hours online, plus scouring my growing library of cookbooks), I discovered that the Bundt cake, which I'd always thought had originated in North America, was actually from Germany. The Bundt cake pans I'd grown up with were an Americanized version of a German pan that was used to make a cake they called Bund-kuchen. I was delighted about my discovery and hoped no one else had blown through as many precious baking hours surfing the net as I had this week. I needed my cake to be unique. And tasty—there was no getting away from the taste test.

Now I had varieties of Bundt cake all over every available kitchen surface and zero clue whether the one with hazelnuts and chocolate tasted better than the lavender and lemon, or if my current attempt—raspberry and white chocolate—was the winner. Clearly, I needed someone with a pulse to help me decide.

I rinsed off my floury hands and called my best friend, Gina. "I need you to come over here, stat," I said, before she'd barely got in a "hello." "It's a cake emergency. And I'll provide wine." She laughed before saying she was up to the challenge and would hop in the car pronto. I thanked my lucky stars for Gina. Even if we couldn't choose the perfect bake, we could gossip and she'd remind me that everything was going to be okay. She was definitely more positive than Mildred.

When I got off the phone, I realized that Mildred had been hovering nearby. She straightened her mobcap and said, "Well, I know when I'm not wanted," and before I could tell her how much I appreciated her advice, she'd faded into the old stone wall. Gateau's little head snapped up, and she flicked her tail as if to say, *Good riddance.* That cat had an appetite for many things, but ghosts were not one of them.

Poor Mildred, such a sensitive spirit. I'd have to think of a way to make it up to her. Maybe something pretty for the kitchen since she spent so much time here. I wondered who would have taken over Broomewode's gift shop now that Eileen was no longer with us. Maybe something in there would suit Mildred's quaint style.

AT THE SOUND of Gina's little Ford Fiesta pulling into my drive, my heart soared. I'd cleaned up the mess in the kitchen and then placed my cakes in a neat row on the old oak table, as if they were about to be judged in the tent. I was going to give Gina the full baking show experience—and hopefully she'd do the same with her judging.

Gina let herself in through the front door, and I rushed over for a massive hug. Her skin smelled of the lavender soap she'd been using since we were teenagers. As a makeup and hair expert on the show, she was always trying out new looks. Today she'd styled her dark hair into soft, shiny waves. "I was thinking of trying it out on you," she confessed when I complimented her. She reached for my long, straight brown hair. "What do you think?"

"I'm so stressed about baking. I can't think about my hair right now."

She put her head to one side. "And viewers want to instantly recognize their favorite bakers. Maybe we'll leave it as is."

"I missed you," I said. I loved having Gina at Broomewode while the baking contest was going on. I could moan and complain to someone who cared. And I did.

Gina laughed. "It's only Tuesday, Pops."

"When you've been making Bundt cake since Sunday evening, three days can seem like a lifetime. Believe me."

I asked her to take a seat at the kitchen table, then cut her thin wedges of each different recipe.

"They all look lovely," Gina said, eyeing her plate greedily.

"I think I've got the decoration down, but it's the taste that's important. Impressing Elspeth and Jonathon is no joke. The flavors have got to be nothing short of perfection. The balance and texture sublime. Otherwise it's curtains for me."

I watched nervously as Gina chomped through each option. I watched her face for feedback, but she refused even to look at me.

Finally, she put her fork down.

"Well?" I asked. "Don't leave me hanging. Which is the best?"

She cleared her throat and sat up straight. "I solemnly declare that the lavender and lemon is the winner."

"You sure?" I asked. "This doesn't have anything to do with your lavender soaps, does it? I know how much you love that scent."

"Nope. It's my impartial verdict. It's delicious. Now cut me another slice."

I let out a huge sigh of relief. I trusted Gina. Now that I'd finally settled on my flavors, I could turn my attention to achieving the perfect crumb. I was reaching for the bottle of wine I'd bribed Gina with when my phone rang.

I picked it up, trying to keep the annoyance out of my voice.

"Oh, hello," a crisp, very British voice said. "I'm so terribly sorry for calling out of the blue like this. My name is Jessica Fowler-Bishop."

I was about to tell her she had the wrong number, as I'd never heard of any Jessica Fowler-Bishop, when she said, "I live in Broomewode Village." Okay, now she had my attention. "Eve at the pub gave me your number. She said you wouldn't mind."

I must have looked baffled because Gina swallowed some cake and mouthed, "Who is it?"

I shook my head, just as nonplussed. Eve was a friend and a fellow witch. She wouldn't give my number out if she didn't think I'd approve. "Um, okay," I said. "And how can I help you?"

"I'm the matron of honor at the wedding of my dear friend Lauren Maycock," she began. It turned out that Lauren's favorite aunt had planned to make the wedding cake, which was a tradition in their family, "But she's ill and now there isn't time."

"That's too bad," I said.

"The whole family is in a complete panic. Worried it's a bad omen or something."

What has this got to do with me?

7

"And that's why I'm calling," Jessica said, as though she sensed my confusion and that I was about to end the call. "Lauren's a huge fan of *The Great British Baking Contest*. We both are. We live in London now, but Lauren's back in the village, staying with her mum while she organizes the wedding. She watches the filming whenever she gets the chance. You're her favorite contestant, Poppy, and if you would make Lauren's wedding cake, it would solve everything."

I was forming my lips into a polite refusal when she kept talking. "I asked Eve about you, and she said you were the nicest contestant on the show. I imagine it would be terrific publicity for you. Please, will you make the wedding cake and turn this disaster into a wonderful gift for my best friend?"

Jessica paused. I looked at Gina, who had almost finished her second piece of cake. She was watching me, obviously waiting for me to get off the phone so I could tell her what was going on. I could feel my eyes widening with disbelief. The show hadn't even aired yet, but a complete stranger knew my name. And my cakes.

"That's very sweet of you to say," I told Jessica, "but I'm a home baker. I'm not qualified for such an important job. Surely you'd be better off with someone who makes wedding cakes for a living. A seasoned professional?"

"I hear what you're saying, but you really are her favorite," Jessica said. "It would mean so much to her on her special day. After all, you only get one chance at the perfect wedding. This would be the icing on the cake, so to speak." She chuckled. "Besides, you have until Friday. Plenty of time."

I gulped. Was this lady for real?

Friday? There was no way I had time to practice for this weekend's filming *and* make a wedding cake.

I started to politely decline, saying that it was only a few days away, when Jessica laughed. "But on the show you make the most incredible creations in only a few hours."

Huh, she'd got me there.

"It's such a fantastic venue, too," Jessica continued. "The Orangery at Broomewode Hall—do you know it? Very swanky. And you'd be invited to the reception, of course. The chefs at Broomewode are doing the catering, so you'd be in for a delicious meal."

I was about to refuse again when the word *Broomewode* sank in. I'd been trying with limited success to find out about my birth mother, who I believed had once worked in the kitchen. With Katie Donegal, the chef at Broomewode Hall, still convalescing in Ireland, this could be a chance for me to get cozy with other people who worked there. Maybe, if I had a legitimate "in," I could ask questions in the kitchen. In spite of the time crunch, this felt like a breakthrough.

I swallowed. Was I really going to do this? I really didn't have time.

"And, of course, the fee will reflect the short notice. Shall we say seven hundred pounds?"

Seven hundred pounds? That was a thousand U.S. dollars. For a cake. I thought of all the extra ingredients I could buy with that money. It would also help with my mortgage this month.

"I suppose I could find a way to squeeze it in this week," I told Jessica after a pause. "After all, I've made three cakes today already—what's another?" I laughed nervously.

Gina started to rise out of her chair, ready to grab the phone away. I batted my hand at her and turned my back.

"Wonderful!" Jessica's voice rang out with pleasure. "Obviously, there's no time for the traditional fruitcake style of wedding cake, so you can do whatever your heart desires, though I did think the wedding cake at Meghan and Harry's wedding was quite lovely."

Of course she did. It was a *royal* wedding.

"Something contemporary but, you know, still tradition-al," she added. "Send me some ideas by email, and we'll work it out."

Oh, great. Vague much? I took Jessica's details, and we made arrangements to meet the day before the wedding.

I hung up, wondering how I'd let this person talk me into making yet another complicated cake when I was slap-bang in the middle of the competition of a lifetime. Clearly this Jessica was a very persuasive woman. With her positive spin on everything and the way she'd gotten me to say yes, I'd bet she was in sales. And if so, she was the top salesperson on her team.

I explained the situation to Gina, who looked at me like I had a Bundt-shaped hole in my head. "You're a glutton for punishment, Pops," she said, wagging a finger at me. "Isn't it enough you're part of the country's most-cherished TV series right now? The whole world watches the baking contest. Now you're putting your chance at victory in jeopardy. Again."

I put my head in my hands while Gina continued to berate me. She was right; I *was* crazy. I was already having trouble keeping up with the competition, and I needed to bring my A-game this week. Not make a wedding cake for a stranger, even if I could use the money.

I told Gina I agreed with everything she was saying, but now I'd finally have a good reason to go into the Broomewode kitchen and try to find more clues about Valerie, who I was certain was my birth mom.

At that, Gina's face softened. She leaned across the table and placed a hand on mine. "I understand," she said quietly. It would have been a touching moment if she hadn't had cake crumbs in her hair.

While I had my phone in hand, I looked up Harry and Meghan's royal wedding cake and groaned. It was an exquisite lemon and elderflower cake, beautifully finished in vanilla buttercream and decorated with sumptuous fresh flowers. It looked simple. And that was part of the genius of the cake baker and decorator. It would have taken hours and hours of concentrated labor to get the flavor and the look exactly right. There was no way I could pull off something that wonderful in the few days I had. *And* become a world-class Bundt maker. If only my witch skills were a little more developed. I could seriously use a bit of magic about now. I touched the amethyst necklace Elspeth had given to me for protection and willed it to start protecting me from my own decisions.

Gina could see that I was alarmed and said we'd figure it out together. I fetched my recipe scrapbook from the shelves. As soon as I'd been accepted onto *The Great British Baking Contest,* I'd begun compiling cake recipes: cutting out magazine segments, interviews and exclusives with celebrity bakers; jotting down word-of-mouth recipes or those that had been passed down to me by friends and friends of friends' families.

"There has to be something in here that we can use as

inspiration," I muttered, turning page after page, waiting for that light-bulb moment to hit.

"What about this one?" I pointed at a photograph of a tiered buttercream cake trimmed with yellow ribbon.

"Coconut and lemon sounds delicious."

She was right. I peered at the page and realized it was one of Elspeth's cakes. Those witchy instincts *must* be kicking in. I could definitely adapt the recipe and turn it into a cake fit for a wedding.

"You should find out the exact color of the bride's dress," Gina suggested, "and the flowers in her bouquet. That way you can match the shade of your buttercream to her dress and decorate it with the same fresh flowers. And hey, presto: a cake fit for the royals...or, in this case, total strangers."

I grinned at Gina. That was an excellent idea. Maybe I *could* pull this off, get closer to the Broomewode staff, and ace the show's challenge this weekend. But I certainly had my work cut out. It was going to be a long week and an even longer weekend.

After Gina left, I put away the Bundt ingredients and began planning a wedding cake. One good thing came of it. When Mildred floated out of the wall, she was a lot happier to see me applying myself to something so traditional.

"I still remember the wedding cake of our beloved queen." She sighed. I knew she meant Victoria. "Beautiful it was, with a dog at Albert's feet, denoting devotion, of course. And two turtledoves at Victoria's. For fidelity. Gunter's did the cake, you know. No, wait a minute. Perhaps that was the royal confectioner. There were several cakes, of course, for Her Majesty's wedding. What a lovely time that was." I let her reminisce about cakes of yore while I reached for the eggs.

CHAPTER 2

I pulled into the grounds of Broomewode Hall with my heart in my mouth. For some reason, I felt super nervous. It might have had something to do with the fact that in the passenger seat was the wedding cake I'd spent the last two days perfecting. It had taken forty-eight hours of deep baking meditation, focusing only on my creaming technique, sifting power, and ingredient sourcing, but the finished product was worth it. While I'd been experimenting with coconut and lemon flavors, I realized that if I made some lavender sugar flowers, then I could do the same decoration for my lavender and lemon Bundt cake, and then all this extra work could help me prepare for the competition. Two flowers, one stone, so to speak.

With a hundred guests to feed, the finished cake was a whopper. I'd carefully iced the layered sponges this morning, but I wouldn't add the finishing touches until tomorrow morning––otherwise the fresh flowers would droop. The first job was to safely deliver the cake to Broomewode Hall's catering staff for storage.

So now here I was, a day before the wedding, with my first ever professional baking job successfully completed, and my first ever legitimate "in" with the staff at Broomewode Hall. It was enough to turn a girl's knees to jelly.

Meanwhile, Gateau had been demoted to riding along in the back, and she was meowing angrily as I brought the car to a stop. "Now, now," I said in hushed tones, "That wasn't so bad." I got out and opened the back door. Could I add cat chauffeur to my string of jobs? Gateau gave me her best cat scowl before jumping down onto the asphalt. A quick stretch and then she scampered off--no doubt to run around the gardens and show me that no one was the boss of her.

The old manor house was as impressive and imposing as ever, the morning sun lending the stone a golden glow. The flowerbeds were full to bursting--Edward, the new gardener, was doing a wonderful job--and the grass had that greener-than-green look I'd come to expect from the meticulously groomed lawns.

I had parked my little car at the delivery area on the northwest side of the house. The staff entrance by the kitchen was slightly less imposing than the front door, but memories of being hustled out of there by Benedict Champney the first time I'd tried to talk to Katie Donegal flooded over me. *Chin up, Poppy,* I commanded. I had a professional right to be in the kitchen today. Cradling the boxed cake like it was a baby, I rang the bell and waited for someone to let me in.

"Just a minute, luvvie," I heard a familiar voice say. "I'm coming."

My heart soared. Was that? Could it be?

The door swung open, and there was Katie Donegal, the Irish cook who'd broken her arm and then gone home to

Ireland. The one who remembered Valerie and then never got a chance to tell me much about the woman I thought was my birth mom.

She wasn't very tall, somewhere around five feet, and a white apron splattered with food stains swamped her round frame.

"Poppy," she said, beaming, her green eyes wide and kind, "the girls told me you'd been roped into this wedding. I didn't believe them at first, what with you still being in the show, but here you are." She peeped into the box with professional curiosity, and I immediately rushed to assure her that the decoration wasn't finished yet. I'd be putting fresh flowers on the cake in the morning.

"It looks very nice. That buttercream is like silk, and the sugar flowers are a treat."

I was thrilled that she liked it. I didn't think she was a woman who gave out praise easily.

"I don't know how you find the time."

I laughed. But seriously, neither did I. "I'm so glad to see you," I said, following Katie as she led me into the bustling kitchen. "The Champneys said you were going to be in Ireland for another few weeks." And by the looks of the cast on her right arm, Katie really shouldn't be in the kitchen.

"Well, I'm supposed to still be there, convalescing," Katie said, sighing, "but I'm not used to being sat about the house. I was staying with my sister, see, and truth be told, I got pretty fed up being a guest in her house. I longed for my own bed, my things around me. I'm a home-bod, really. Besides"—she gestured at the chaos around us—"I missed being in the kitchen. It's where I belong."

The sound of metal spoons clanging against pots and

pans and the clunk of heavy knives on wooden chopping boards filled the air. The kitchen was uncomfortably warm, the air thick with steam and fragrant with roasting smells. "I don't know if you've had the pleasure of meeting Ms. Jessica Fowler-Bishop, but it's nothing but the finest of everything for her best friend's wedding." She shook her head. "And as for talking you into making the wedding cake because you're a television star, well, I don't know what the world's coming to. I told her we could make her a lovely cake but nothing would do, she had to have Poppy Wilkinson. The bride's taken a shine to you, she has, and that was the end of it."

So there had been other options. Jessica Fowler-Bishop had made it sound as though I were the only hope. It was flattering, but she hadn't been entirely truthful. Well, so long as she hadn't lied about the seven hundred quid, I'd get over myself.

Broomewode Hall might be hundreds of years old, but their modern industrial kitchen was the perfect place to prepare for a wedding. I watched as Katie one-handedly cleared a space on the kitchen table, maneuvering the long wooden canapé boards and seemingly endless piles of chopped herbs until there was a gap large enough for my cake box. "You pop that giant thing there while I have a think about where is cool enough in this sweaty kitchen to store the cake till later."

I quickly set the box down, glad to get the weight off my arms and almost bursting with the questions I'd wanted to ask Katie for the past four weeks. I'd accepted this job for a reason. And now I was being rewarded. I hoped Katie could be the key to me uncovering the truth about Valerie. *One step at a time, Poppy,* I told myself. *Keep cool and don't blow it.*

As Katie chattered on about her sister, I took in the bustling scene around us. There were six members of staff in the kitchen, each with their own duties. Two were furiously chopping. Two were assembling complicated-looking layers of filo pastry. Another woman was culling strawberries, and one was stirring something on the industrial-size stove. It was all go, go, go. The woman who'd taken Katie's place in the kitchen shot me a despairing look, as if to say, *Are you seriously here to interrupt all this work?* I made a helpless gesture toward the cake.

"Katie, why don't you and the baker take the cake into the back pantry," the woman suggested, raising an eyebrow. We were obviously getting in her way, but some alone time with Katie would give me the perfect opportunity to finally quiz her Broomewode knowledge.

Katie shot me a devious look and whispered, "She thinks she's in charge."

I picked up the cake box and followed Katie along a narrow hallway to the pantry. As we walked, I remembered how cagey she'd been when I'd last asked her about Valerie. At first, she'd claimed not to recall a woman with that name, then she'd changed her tune and said perhaps there had been someone called Valerie who'd worked at Broomewode Hall more than twenty years ago but that she'd not been there long before she left abruptly, with no forwarding address. When I'd pressed her for more details, she said that sometimes people didn't want to be found and that it was kinder to respect their wishes. Was Katie truly being kind and respecting Valerie's desire to disappear? Or was she helping to cover something up? Like a pregnancy. I knew I was going to have to tread carefully when it came to questioning Katie some more. I didn't want to overstep and have her clam up on me again.

I decided that rather than bring up the name Valerie, I'd ask Katie about the woman wearing the shawl in the dining room painting. That shawl was the one thing that connected me with Broomewode, as I'd been wrapped in that hand-knitted shawl when I'd been found in a Somerset apple box outside the Philpotts' bakery.

Katie slid open a set of doors. The pantry was a perfect square, with a stone floor and brick walls. It was cool without being refrigerator-cold. Perfect. Floor-to-ceiling shelves were filled with produce. The Champneys certainly ate well, or maybe this was for the wedding. We stepped inside, and a wave of cool air rushed over me.

"It's always nice and cool in here," Katie said, leaning against the brick walls. "It's the flagstone floor. In the old days, before fridges were invented, the staff used to keep the perishables in here. Imagine having to leave your butter in here and pray to the gods that it didn't turn into a sticky yellow pool before the next breakfast." She gestured to a space on the shelves, and I set the cake box next to a row of jam jars where it wouldn't be bumped.

I chuckled. I told Katie how all week long I'd thanked my professional mixer for its dexterous whisks and plentiful speed settings. I had no idea how people had the patience to cream sugar and butter by hand or whisk batter without modern technology. Who had the time? Naturally, I couldn't tell her how Mildred claimed no machine could match a proper cook's touch, but that was pure jealousy talking.

"And how is the competition going? Are you finding

enough time to practice?" Katie asked kindly. "Seems like you've lots on your cake plate." She laughed.

I took a deep breath and prepared myself to pick Katie's brain. I explained how I'd been super busy trying to balance being in the competition while still working. I told her all about my "commission" to sketch the interiors of manor houses for a design magazine—just a slight bend of the truth: my real job had been to sketch flowers and plants for a hard-back book about the English country garden.

"I don't know where you find the energy, dearie," Katie said. "Just a couple of days back here and my feet are already giving me jip."

I expressed sympathy for her aching feet and then launched into my plan. I told her that Lord Frome had invited me to sketch their dining room and I'd been intrigued by a beautiful oil painting hanging on the wall. "It's of a grand lady, and she's wearing the most unusual shawl. I was drawn to its pattern but didn't manage to capture it properly in my sketch. Any chance you'd know who made it or where the shawl came from?"

I decided not to tell Katie that I thought the shawl had been given to Valerie. After she'd been so skittish last time I'd brought up that name, a little circumnavigating the truth was going to be necessary.

Katie suddenly busied herself moving a jar of rhubarb jam that had ended up among the quince jelly, and that seemed to take all her attention before she turned and looked at me blankly. "Can't say I know which painting you're talking about. I don't pay much attention to the art here," she said, shrugging. "It's all the same to me—haven't got 'the eye,' as they say." But I noticed she was standing a little straighter, more alert than before, and her forehead was creasing ever so slightly. Was she pretending to ignorance even as she knew how that shawl had gone from the former countess to baby me?

Katie nodded toward the door, and we walked back through the narrow hallway. I had to persevere with my line of questioning before we got back to the busy kitchen and were overheard. I'd spent two solid days on that wedding cake, and this was my payoff. I didn't want to blow it.

"I was really hoping you'd be able to help me out about that painting," I said. "I have to provide details for the magazine about artifacts in stately homes. Do you think we could go into the main house quickly and look in the dining room? It might jog your memory. Maybe we could find a signature on the painting so I could research the artist."

I could see that she was about to decline, so I put on my best puppy-dog expression and stressed how much I needed this job. Every detail I could gather was important.

Her kind eyes softened. "Lord and Lady Frome are out this morning, so if we're quick, we can get in and out of the main house without them thinking we're snooping."

I thanked her and followed along the narrow corridor and up the servants' staircase to the main house. Despite her broken arm, Katie moved with ease and speed. She obviously knew this house like the back of her own hand.

Once we'd entered the wide hall on the main floor, Katie looked around, checking that the coast was clear, before opening the dining room door. "Let's be quick. They can't survive for long in the kitchen without me."

I stepped inside the lovely room. It was as I remembered it. There were the enormous bay windows, framed by heavy tapestried curtains woven through with gold. The cream wallpaper reached up to the paneled ceilings, which were bordered by a deep red runner. The antique dining table was a rich mahogany color, matching the sideboards and display cabinets. It was such a beautiful, thoughtfully decorated room.

But then I saw something that made my heart stop its admiring flutter. "I don't understand," I murmured.

"What's that, dearie?" Katie asked.

I pointed at the far wall, where a rectangular patch of cream wallpaper was paler than the rest. "It's gone," I said, shaking my head. "The painting's gone."

"Are you sure it was in here?" Katie asked. "There's plenty of old paintings in this place. They're everywhere you look, really. In the hallways, the bedrooms, in the bathrooms…"

"No. It was here. Look, you can see where it hung." Before I finished speaking, the door opened behind me, and I spun round. It was Tilbury, the snooty butler. His portly frame was encased in its usual pristine formal black jacket, the white shirt stiff with starch. And, as usual, he seemed pretty put out by my presence at Broomewode Hall.

Tilbury sniffed, looking from my guilty face to Katie's. "Mrs. Donegal. Is there something I can help you with?" His tone was cold, and he barely acknowledged my presence.

I didn't want poor Katie getting in trouble when I was the one who'd begged her to bring me here, hoping she'd remember that painting. I swallowed. "I'm afraid that's my fault," I said. "Lord Frome invited me to sketch the dining room last week as part of an important magazine commission. There was a detail I couldn't quite capture in the moment, so I twisted Katie's arm to accompany me to the dining room for another look."

Tilbury raised one bushy eyebrow. "Twisted her arm?"

Oh, Poppy. What a choice of words.

Was he making a joke? If he was, he had the best poker face I'd ever seen. "Sorry, unfortunate turn of phrase. She was kind enough to show me the way."

"I would have thought, Miss Wilkinson, that you already knew your way around the place quite well enough."

Okay, wise guy, gimme a break here.

I flashed my best, *Hey I'm just a curious American* smile and shrugged. "What happened to the painting that was hanging there?" I pointed to the blank spot where the picture had been only a week ago.

Tilbury turned and looked at where I was pointing, and I could have sworn he did a double take. Then he looked down his nose at me. "Some of the paintings have been taken for cleaning."

Oh, no! I really wanted to show Katie that painting and look at it again myself. "Any idea when it will be returned?"

He looked at me as though I were a cockroach he was about to stamp on. Did they teach that look in butler school? "I really couldn't say, miss." Tilbury took a step toward the door and opened it a little wider. Subtle much?

"Right then. We'll be heading back to the kitchen," Katie said. I couldn't help but notice she looked worried.

As I followed Katie out, I felt terrible. Had I gotten her into trouble with Tilbury? That was the last thing I wanted. I did, however, check out the walls of the hallway, and they were as crammed with paintings as the last time I'd been here. I wondered how many paintings had gone for cleaning.

Was it a coincidence that the painting I was interested in had conveniently disappeared?

I didn't know what to say to make it better, so I asked Katie about the wedding preparations, what kind of food they were serving, and what she could tell me about the bride and groom. She immediately perked up and launched into an anecdote about the happy couple, how handsome they were, and how nice it was to have some of the younger people return to the village to celebrate their matrimony. "So many others choose to have their weddings in la-di-da venues in the city. But if you ask me, not even a fancy London hotel has a patch on the beauty of the Orangery here in old Broomewode."

I made all the right noises as she talked—or at least I hoped I did—but my mind was focused on the painting. Katie obviously knew something about Valerie that she wasn't prepared to share; her body language kept giving her away. But I couldn't dance around the subject anymore. It was time to bite the bullet. If I was going to get Katie to talk, she was going to have to trust me. Maybe I'd have to share more of my motivations for Katie to see why this was so important.

I reached out to stop Katie from opening the kitchen door. "Before we go back in, could I show you these?"

I took my phone from my back pocket and lowered my voice because, frankly, who knew who might be lurking about, eavesdropping in this place. "I took a couple of photos of the painting to help with my sketch. It's not the same as seeing the painting up close, of course. But do you remember I asked you about a woman called Valerie last time we saw each other? Well, I think Valerie might have been given this very shawl. It's a long shot, but it might help me trace her. Do you remember anything at all about the shawl?"

Katie's sweet expression disappeared as she looked up from my phone, and a furrow appeared in her brow. "Dearie, I really don't recall anything about this shawl, pretty as it is. The colors are lovely."

My heart sank.

Katie looked back at the phone again. "She was a beauty, wasn't she? The countess, I mean. That portrait must have been painted before the tragedy." Katie shook her head. "What a sad, sad business. All that wasted youth. Her son. Her pride and joy."

I nodded. "Eve told me about the riding accident. How he was thrown from his horse and fell from the cliff top. I've had nightmares about it, actually. A terrible way to go."

Katie agreed and sighed. "Truth be told, the countess never got over it. She was a kind lady, generous with her words and with her time. Very caring. It broke her spirit when the young viscount died. She was heartbroken."

I told Katie that many people in the village remembered her fondly.

Katie's eyes misted over, and she seemed lost in memories of the past. I decided to act and ask one final time if she knew anything about Valerie.

At her name, Katie's head snapped back up. She looked at me kindly, obviously feeling sorry for the girl with the one-track mind, and I could see her own mind ticking over, contemplating something, weighing some odds which I couldn't fathom. *Please just tell me what you know,* I thought— trying to invoke some kind of telepathy. *It's so important.*

My telepathy attempt must have worked because Katie

took a deep breath and then lowered her voice another notch. "I can see you're on some kind of journey, Poppy," she said. "For reasons I don't even want to know, this woman has become important to you. But remember what I said before? About how some people don't want to be found? Well, Valerie made it quite clear that she wanted to disappear. Completely."

"Please," I half-whispered. "Any information would be so helpful."

Katie sighed. "The poor girl got herself into trouble." She patted her plump belly. A small puff of flour rose into the air.

Finally: the truth. I'd got Katie to crack and spill. Did she have an inkling that *I* was the reason Valerie's belly had swollen? I thought, perhaps, she'd guessed and for some reason didn't want to let on. As with the missing painting, I wondered why.

"Do you have any idea who the father was?" I asked, trying to slow my heartbeat. I needed to get a grip on my mounting excitement. *Hold it together, Poppy.*

But Katie just shook her head. "Could have been one of the village lads. She used to go to London on her days off. I expect she had a chap there. She never said. Kept her thoughts to herself, did Valerie. And one night, she simply disappeared."

"Are you certain you don't have her full name written anywhere?" With a first name, there wasn't much I could do, but a surname would really help. I'd tried online searches and joined ancestry groups, but I had so little information, I'd never progressed in my search. I'd learned more in the last few weeks at Broomewode than I'd managed in the years before it. I felt tantalizingly close.

She looked at me intently. "Leave it be, love."

I thought she'd say more, but the kitchen door flung open, and the chef appeared, gripping a wooden spoon as if her life depended on it. "Need more butter for the Hollandaise sauce."

Katie looked as though the woman had struck her with the wooden spoon. "Making the Hollandaise already? But the wedding's not until tomorrow." She puffed up like a broody hen. "I never make a Hollandaise sauce in advance."

The woman pursed up her mouth and leaned back. "There are quite a few new techniques since your day." As rude as she was, I felt like I was back in my kitchen with Mildred exclaiming that everything was better in the old days.

I excused myself and left them to it. No doubt they'd be slinging barely veiled insults at each other for some time. I'd be curious to taste the Hollandaise tomorrow and decide for myself.

I was grateful that Katie had finally come out and told me that Valerie had been pregnant when she left. I was all but certain that Valerie was my mom. But as to the question of who my father was or where he and Valerie might have gone, well, that was another mystery I was going to have to solve. Clearly without any more help from the Broomewode cook.

Why was Katie so insistent that I "leave it alone"? What did she know? Maybe my father was in jail or something and she'd wanted to shield me. I definitely got the feeling she knew more than she was willing to tell me.

Again, I wondered why.

CHAPTER 3

I exited Broomewode Hall through the servants' entrance, my head buzzing with thoughts of my birth dad. The blue sky had acquired some cotton-wool clouds while I'd been inside, and now the manicured lawns were dappled with diagonal stripes of sunlight. I stepped out onto the thick, springy green grass and inhaled the floral scent that was carried on the breeze. I checked my watch: It was only eleven a.m.––plenty of time to gather the fresh flowers I needed to complete the wedding cake decoration. Then I could make my way to the wedding venue, check that the blooms matched with the bridal color theme, and see where my cake would be displayed. My wedding duties were almost complete. Relieved was an understatement.

I strode across the lawns, in search of a couple of puffy white peonies or perhaps some delicate white roses from the abundant gardens. I wanted my cake to look like a dream–– the childhood dream come true for an excited bride, no less.

It was a risk thinking I'd find the blooms I wanted on the

estate, but I was certain I'd find something that would work. Broomewode's gardens were pretty amazing.

In the distance, I heard the faint sound of a lawnmower, and as I turned the corner, there was Edward, the young gardener, mowing the lawns. He had his head bent in concentration, and from the faint white lines I could see dangling from his ears, he had earphones in, too. I decided to say hello later.

As I walked, the birdsong and the beauty of the landscape, along with Katie's confirmation of what I'd felt in my heart about Valerie, left me with a deep sense of purpose and appreciation for where I was and what I was doing. I had to admit that after my mediocre bakes last weekend, I had felt a little glum this week. Although the sun had been shining, my mood had remained gray, like looking out across a river on a rainy day. But now I felt hopeful, like anything was possible. I could find out where I'd come from, bake a killer Bundt cake this weekend, and learn more about my witchy heritage from Elspeth. Plus, a wedding was imminent, and nothing felt more hopeful to me than two people promising themselves to each other, even if it was two strangers. Despite the bad timing, I was flattered to have been asked to make my first professional wedding cake. I was pleased with the cake, and with the addition of some fresh flowers, I'd make sure that the bride and groom were really wowed by my efforts.

Following the now familiar pebbled path, I hunted for perfect blooms. Over the past few weeks, I'd become well acquainted with Broomewode Hall's delightful garden, and I was sure that I'd seen my favorite floribunda roses earlier. It was the "blue eyes" specimen that I was especially interested in. They had wide, delicate pale-pink blooms with an

28

exquisite mauve-blue center. Next to some fresh white peonies, or perhaps even some deeper magenta pinks, they'd look beautiful––and a good fit for the champagne-blush bridesmaid dresses.

And there they were. Nestled among a bed of quite ordinary-looking white roses were the "blue eyes" I was after. I crouched down and inhaled their scent. With any luck, the bride would have blue eyes, and I could spin a charming story about the rose's name. I was really getting the hang of this wedding lark.

I was hunting about for the perfect specimen when I felt a set of eyes boring into my back.

Turning round, I had to suppress a groan. What bad luck. Who worse to catch me picking his flowers than the young lord of the manor? "Hello, Benedict," I said, pulling myself up from the ground. I held my head high, despite having been caught red-handed taking flowers from his family garden.

"Poppy." He was wearing a crumpled pale blue linen shirt and indigo jeans––more casual and carefree than his usual style.

I dusted down my hands, keeping a firm grasp on my burgeoning bouquet.

"I see another week has passed and you've yet to learn the meaning of the words *private property.*" He smiled as he spoke, and his tone was gently teasing. Could it be true? Did Benedict Champney have a sense of humor?

I explained about the lemon and coconut wedding cake I'd been busy making, how I'd been called upon out of the blue, and that I'd just dropped the cake off to Katie in the kitchen. "The flowers here will complete the cake decorations perfectly." I lowered my voice and made a sweeping gesture at the grounds. "I didn't think you'd mind me taking one or two for a *community* wedding," I said.

Benedict pulled a pocket knife from his jeans. For a wild moment, I wondered if he was going to chase me off the property, but instead, he bent down and cut a stem of the most beautiful peony I'd ever seen. Its petals were the palest yellow, just opening out from a tight bud to reveal its soft, rippling petals.

"It's an herbaceous peony called Lemon Chiffon—quite fitting for a wedding, no? I imagine the wedding dress has some chiffon somewhere, and lemon for your cake."

I stared at Benedict, lost for words. The bloom was perfect, and there was something courtly in the way he offered me the pale yellow peony.

I mumbled a thank you, feeling suddenly out of my depth, but I needn't have worried. Benedict had already slipped back into his usual formal self. He cleared his throat. "Do feel free to take a few more," he said, suddenly sounding brisk, "but be sure to tell the bridal party where they came from. We could do with some positive press."

He turned back toward the manor house. I was wondering what had made Benedict so self-conscious all of sudden when I saw Edward looking over in my direction, hands poised on the lawnmower but not moving. I raised a hand in hello, and he waved in return. I was about to go over to say hello when Edward started up the mower again and continued powering across the grass. Hopefully I'd see him in the pub later.

I took the newly generous Benedict at his word and quickly picked a few more roses and peonies before heading back to my car to drive the short distance to the inn. With all the rushing around that I'd had to do this week, I'd finally managed the art of packing light. I took my suitcase from the car and went straight to the bar to see if I could score my usual room.

Inside, the early lunch rush was just beginning, and couples and groups filled the soft red banquettes that lined the wall of the pub, pints of shandy and glasses of white wine resting on the deep mahogany tables. To my delight, Eve was behind the bar. I caught her eye and grinned. Was it weird that the inn was beginning to feel more like home than my actual cottage? Every detail of the room was familiar to me: the long-stemmed red candles in empty wine bottles waiting to be lit; the hunting prints that hung on the walls; the old oak bar with its row of pumps for pulling pints of ale, wineglasses hanging upside down from hooks above them; the bottles of liquor lined up in front of a mirror. It really was cozy and inviting. My home away from home.

Before I'd even said hello, Eve leaned across the bar, pecked my cheek hello and pressed the key to my usual room into the palm of my hand. "Already knew you were coming early, Poppy," she said with a grin.

I touched my finger to the side of my nose, as if to say, *witchy intuition,* but Eve just laughed.

"Jessica Fowler-Bishop. Now there is a woman with some serious powers of persuasion. I hope you didn't mind that I passed on your number. Somehow I agreed to it without even realizing what was happening. I actually thought you'd turn the job down. I'm glad you didn't so I can see you a day early."

"Me too." Now that the cake was done, I was happy I'd taken on the job. It had given me some of my confidence back to bake a cake knowing it would be eaten by happy people, not scrutinized and criticized.

"Some of the wedding guests are staying at the inn." She gestured at the more rowdy tables who were already tucking into plates of food. "Jessica's been boasting about how she persuaded you to make the cake. I can't believe you agreed to more work while still filming the show. You must be a little loopy...like the rest of us."

"Loopy and exhausted sounds about right." I grimaced and then smiled. "Honestly, I don't know if it was her smooth-talking talents or my own stupidity which won out in the end. But I've managed to pull it off. The cake is a beauty—if I can say so myself. Besides, you know me: anything to get me closer to the mysterious inner workings of Broomewode Hall."

Eve's brow furrowed ever so slightly, and her eyes clouded over with concern. "I thought that might have something to do with it. You must be careful, Poppy. The Champneys are a private bunch, and you're already on their radar. Make sure you don't rub them up the wrong way."

I'd never seen Eve look worried that way before. I promised that I'd be careful. The warning note I'd received the week before last flashed back into my mind. I hadn't forgotten its words, but now they raced back to me:

Dearest Poppy,
You are in terrible danger. You shouldn't be here. I'm
begging you: Do something to get yourself voted off of the
show next week. Otherwise I fear it will be too late. Please
heed my words.

I couldn't believe that I still hadn't managed to figure out who had sent the note. Maybe I could put Gerry back onto the job this week. Not that he'd been much help so far, but I believed in second chances.

With my luggage in one hand, key and flowers in the other, I climbed the stairs and braced myself for the inevitability of finding Gerry floating about in my room.

But to my relief, the room was ghost-free. Nothing but a wonderfully made bed, stacked with plump cushions, an empty armchair, and an empty wardrobe ready and waiting to receive my capsule collection of weekend attire.

I let out a long sigh, exhausted from the busy week, and said a silent prayer as I touched my amethyst necklace, hoping that I'd somehow find the inner strength to bake my little socks off this weekend.

I took a water glass from the bathroom, filled it up to give my bunch of wedding blooms a nice long drink, and set the bunch on the windowsill.

Now to unpack. I was hanging a dress in the wardrobe when a white freckled arm floated through the door.

Well, that didn't last long.

"Pops!" Gerry said, as limb by limb he emerged until his shock of spiky red hair appeared. "What a pleasant surprise. I wasn't expecting you until tomorrow."

So what are you doing here now? I wanted to ask but instead swallowed down the words and greeted him with a big smile. I explained about the wedding cake, how I'd been contacted out of the blue by an old Broomewode local who was a fan of the show.

"Ooh, Pops, that's so cool. This could be a whole new chapter for you. You could have your own business. I can see

33

the sign outside your studio already: Poppy Wilkinson: Wedding Cake Master Baker. Cakes for the discerning bride."

I chuckled and put my hands on my hips as if he was a naughty schoolboy getting a telling off––which, come to think of it, was a pretty a good analogy for my relationship with Gerry. "Now don't let your imagination run too wild. I'm barely scraping by in the competition right now. I don't think anyone is going to take me seriously unless I can turn things around this week."

"Just keep your head in the game, Pops. No more gallivanting around the village and poking your nose in where it doesn't belong." He came closer and tapped me on the nose, though of course I didn't feel anything but a touch of cold as though I'd put only the tip of my nose outside the window on a cool winter's night. "That pert little nose needs to be stuck in a cookbook or a canister of flour all weekend, right?"

Hmm, I hated to admit it, but Gerry had a good point. I knew I would be taking a little me time, though, at least to pop in to the wedding reception, since I was invited and I wanted to see how the cake was received. So I asked him how his week had been, whether he'd gotten more comfortable with his spirit life.

He looked ridiculously pleased with himself. "I've been working on my poltergeist skills. Check this out."

Gerry closed his eyes and screwed up his face. I had to stifle a giggle. I watched him, bemused, for almost a full minute before I noticed the dress I'd hung up was making its way from the wardrobe to the bed. I let out a long whistle, and Gerry's eyes snapped open and the dress dropped to the floor.

"Wow-wee," I said, genuinely impressed. "That was amazing." I decided not to give him a hard time about dumping my freshly ironed dress on the carpet. "You've come leaps and bounds."

Gerry grinned and then bowed. "It takes a lot of energy, but I'm getting better for sure."

Clearly he didn't have enough energy left to pick my dress up from the floor. I retrieved it and put it in the wardrobe. When I turned back, Gerry had spirited one of the blue-eyes roses from the water glass, and now it was hanging in midair.

"I see you have an admirer." He put his hands on his hips. "I only hope the chap is worthy of you."

I snorted and plucked the rose out of the air and put it back with the rest. "Very clever," I said.

"Why don't you try moving things, Poppy?"

"If you hadn't noticed, I'm not a poltergeist. I'm not even dead."

"I know you're not. But you *are* a witch. I bet you could move things if you tried."

Actually, I did have a new trick I'd been working on, but I wasn't sure if I was ready to share my burgeoning witchcraft skills with Gerry. I'd hoped that Elspeth would be my first audience, but hey, I'd take what I could get.

"Okay. Watch this," I commanded.

I walked over to my suitcase and pulled out a beeswax candle and a ceramic dish I'd brought from home. I put the candle on the windowsill and breathed in slowly. Unlike Gerry, I didn't close my eyes but instead narrowed their focus until only the candle's wick filled my view. An electric fizz coursed through my body, beginning in my belly and reaching out to my toes and fingertips. I buzzed with the vibrations. And a few seconds later, the candle sparked into life and a golden wavy flame rose from the wick.

"Blimey," Gerry said. "Now that's a neat trick."

"Not a cheap trick--pure magic," I said, blowing out the flame. And it was true. Even I didn't know how I'd managed to pull it off. My new talent had revealed itself entirely by accident earlier in the week. I'd been trying to relight my old gas stove, which had given up the ghost (so to speak) after too many rounds of baking. I'd been so focused on getting the darn thing going again that it had sprung to life seemingly by itself, but as it did, my whole body fizzed with that familiar magic electricity. And so I tried it again with a candle, staring hard at the wick with all my concentration. And presto—a flame.

"I reckon it's the same skill to move things around," Gerry said. "Come here. Try lifting the rose out of the glass. Just concentrate on moving the stem first. Visualize it rising out of the water and into the air. You can keep your eyes open if you like. Focus, but remember to breathe."

I listened to Gerry's voice, which had taken on the dulcet tones of a charlatan hypnotist, and tried to follow his instructions.

Nothing. The thing wouldn't budge.

"Don't give up, Pops," Gerry said softly. "Just keep imagining the stem rising."

I stayed with it. In my head, I said a spell.

> *Let this rose float free*
> *Up in the air without gravity*
> *So I will, so mote it be.*

I was beginning to realize that a lot of spell work was about focus. I was pouring every ounce of concentration I had into moving the rose...and then without knowing I was doing it, I added a hand movement, my finger pointing at the bloom. The rose lifted into the air. Just an inch or so, but there it was, hovering out of the water.

"Yessss!" Gerry said. "Don't stop now. You can go higher than that."

I narrowed my eyes and willed the thing to go higher. The words *You can do this* formed a loop in my brain. *You can do this,* I heard my mom say. *You can do this,* I heard my dad say. *You can do this,* I heard Elspeth say...And then the rose flew out of the vase and landed on the floor.

"Whoa," Gerry said, impressed. "I haven't ever managed to *throw* objects about like that."

"I didn't mean to," I replied, rushing over to inspect the flower. Phew. All petals in their rightful place. No crushed stems. I gently returned it to the vase. "I had no idea I could levitate a flower."

"Now that you know your own strength, you're going to need to apply it to the competition this weekend, Pops. Levitate your standing in the competition, or you'll be going home."

Thanks for reminding me.

"Use that focus to improve your baking. And now for a trick you definitely can't do," Gerry said. And he floated through the wall.

I laughed and called out goodbye. "And next time you visit, please knock," I added. He chuckled from the next room. I did hope it was empty—I didn't want anyone here thinking I'd lost my mind.

I was about to finish the unpacking Gerry had interrupted when I heard a plaintive meow at the window.

I lifted the sash window and let Gateau in. "Perfect timing, little one," I said. "You just missed your least favorite ghost."

Gateau looked up at me, unamused, and then curled up in the armchair. I stroked her silky black fur. "Well, Gerry may be a clown, but he had a point about getting my focus back on track."

I was finished unpacking when my phone beeped. A text message informed me that Jessica, the bride, and bridesmaids were decorating the venue. I'd asked for some of the bridal ribbon to loop among the fresh flowers, and she told me to come up now and get it. Perfect. I might as well deliver these flowers at the same time so everything was on site for the morning's final cake prep.

Besides, I wanted to meet the bride who was going to celebrate her wedding with my cake.

CHAPTER 4

*O*utside, the clouds had cleared, and the midday sun was high in the pale blue sky.

I was excited to see the Broomewode Orangery. I'd read a bit about them when Jessica told me that's where the wedding would be held. Orangeries had become popular in the 18th century as ornate greenhouses built to grow tropical fruit during the cold winter months—though how anyone could manage to grow tropical fruit here even in the summer months would have required a level of optimism I couldn't even imagine. Some of the existing orangeries had been turned into exclusive wedding venues and were coveted for their glorious high ceilings and light-filled reception rooms. I had to admit that I was pretty excited to see such a lovely wedding venue up close. The last wedding I'd been to was for a second cousin on my dad's side, held in the family's back-yard. BBQ chicken and mac and cheese.

From the enthusiastic way Jessica had talked about this wedding on the phone, I knew this one would be a huge step up. The matron of honor planned things with serious attention to detail—and, according to some online reviews I'd read, the food would be nothing less than decadent with the Broomewode Hall catering team behind the menu.

When I reached the Orangery, I felt my jaw drop. Either side of me, undulating lawns, trimmed into neat stripes, stretched out toward the countryside. The driveway was overseen by topiary pyramid trees potted in rows of smart charcoal planters, leading up to a beautiful white building, the sunbeams making the panes of glass sparkle. To its right was a gentle, trickling stream, with a pretty ornate white bridge that I could see was the perfect spot for staging wedding-day photographs.

The Orangery was in keeping with the stunning Georgian architecture I'd come to expect at Broomewode. The windows were as long as they were wide, and a huge skylight covered the west side of the building. Wisteria had been trained on a lattice surrounding the entrance, and its boughs hung low so that the purple petals seemed to be reaching for the potted plants that flanked the door. I went to take a closer look.

On the terrace was a neat row of chairs arranged in a split semicircle. The aisle was fringed by rows of tall vases filled with beautiful pink and white flower arrangements. They faced a trellis arch, wound with white roses, under which the happy couple would say their nuptials. What a gorgeous setup. The bride must be thrilled. I could see movement inside and went to find someone who'd show me where the cake would go later and to put my lovely blooms in some much-needed water.

Two women were in the corner, one holding a ladder, the other at the top hanging streams of blush-pink ribbon.

I called out hello and introduced myself as the cake maker (I admit I blushed with pride at that), and the women turned to face me.

The one at the top of the ladder climbed nimbly down and came toward me. She had long, straight, honey-blond hair, with a few subtle highlights framing her heart-shaped face. Her hazel eyes were clear and bright, the gorgeous color emphasized by a swipe of golden eye shadow. The apples of her cheeks were flushed pink, and her lips were painted a frosty pink that matched the ribbon still clutched in her hand. She was wearing a loose-fitting white jumpsuit with deep pockets, her skin tanned and smooth. Around her throat lay a chunky black statement necklace.

"It's you!" she exclaimed, rushing over. "You're Poppy. I'm Lauren, the bride." She giggled. "I love saying those words. It's so nice to meet you, Poppy. You saved my wedding day. I couldn't believe it when Jessica told me she'd snagged a star from The Great British Baking Contest, and my favorite one to boot. What an honor." She gave me a bear hug.

I laughed, flattered. "Not a star at all, just an ordinary American with a sweet tooth. It's really my honor to be asked." I tucked my white poplin shirt back into my jeans, wishing I could be as effortlessly glamorous as the bride-to-be looked in her ensemble.

The other woman joined us and introduced herself as Jessica, matron of honor. "I'm the one who hired you. Lauren was beside herself, so you saved her day." She was wearing wide-legged russet trousers and a mustard V-neck T-shirt. A pile of rich brown curls had been twisted into a loose bun on top of her head. Her eye makeup was bold: a liquid black line ending with a flick, heavy black mascara, her arched brows brushed up and defined with brown pencil. The inner corners of her eyes glittered with white sparkle, and her generous mouth had been painted a soft peach. She stuck out her hand and then shook mine vigorously. It was clear who was the boss here.

"My pleasure," I said.

"Welcome, welcome," Jessica said. "We're putting the finishing touches to the reception room. There's a lot of work still to be done to get this place up to scratch."

I looked around me, confused. To my eyes, this place was a palace. Glass roof lanterns and a row of French patio doors meant that the room was flooded with bright light. In each corner was a living orange tree—a nice touch. The parquet floor was polished and shining, and arranged at intervals were round tables, draped with blush-pink table-cloths and set up for a three-course sit-down meal. To my delight, a bouquet of pink and white peonies spilled out from elegant crystal vases in the center of each table. My cake decorations would match them perfectly. Who could want more?

I said as much to Jessica, who didn't agree. "Oh, it could be much better. And I intend to fix every little detail. Take the chairs, for example. They're too close together. We don't want our guests elbowing each other as they tuck into an expensive filet mignon, do we? And what about these orange trees? There's no fruit on them. I'm trying to arrange some oranges to be stitched on there somehow. But none of the staff here are being forthcoming with solutions." She shook her head disapprovingly, and her lips curled in disdain.

"Oh, Jessica," Lauren said with affection, "you're such a perfectionist. I couldn't wish for a more beautiful spot."

"You deserve the very best," Jessica quickly retorted.

I witnessed this exchange in a state of mild terror. Jessica was even more demanding in real life than she'd been on the phone. And she seemed a lot more particular than the bride. Lauren seemed very chill for a woman on the eve of her wedding. I hoped she approved of my cake.

"So Poppy," Lauren said. "I'm rooting for you to win the show. Broomewode is a small village, and you're quite the celebrity in these parts." She lowered her voice and whispered excitedly, "I watch a bit of the filming whenever I can, and you're definitely going to be a finalist. Maybe you'll win the whole competition."

"Thanks." I only hoped I didn't get sent home on her wedding weekend. How awkward would that be? Getting me to bake her wedding cake the same week I flunked out of the show?

"Where's the cake? I'm dying to see it."

I told her that it was safely stored in the cool Broomewode Hall pantry. The catering team would deliver it tomorrow morning along with the rest of the banquet. "I don't want you to see it before the fresh flowers are on it and I've put the final decorating touches on it. I really want you to be surprised."

"I understand," she said. "I can't wait."

"Perfect," Jessica said. "When the catering team comes early tomorrow morning, they'll set the cake on that table over there in the corner. As I told you on the phone, we've managed to borrow a silver cake stand from Broomewode Hall, too."

I smiled. None of my cakes had ever been plated on silver before. How had Jessica managed to wangle that favor from the tight-lipped (and equally tight-pursed) Champneys? Even as I was wondering, Jessica said, "I explained that Lauren's a local girl, and the catering manager put me in touch with the family butler, and he managed to get us a piece of the family silver." She laughed. "That's my 'something borrowed.'"

She waited expectantly, and Lauren gushed, "That's fantastic, Jessica. No one ever had a better matron of honor." I realized that Jessica was one of those people who needed praise as much as she needed control, so I echoed Lauren. "What a wonderful favor. You really have a way with people."

She smiled then. "I do. Never taking no for an answer is my secret."

"And baking winning cakes is yours," Lauren said, turning back to me. "Lemon and coconut is going to be so good. Much more contemporary than my poor aunt's fruitcake, which she's been making for fifty years at least for Christmas and family weddings. It's the same recipe."

"I'm happy to offer a change." And, looking around, I thought the cake was going to fit in perfectly with the décor, and based on me and Gina taste-testing, the cake was going to be delicious.

Lauren beamed. "It's going to be absolutely gorgeous. I'm so lucky to have such a wonderful team around me." She prodded Jessica playfully. "Especially you, Jess. I'm so grateful to you for making this all happen. You've run the planning like a pro. You should really make this your day job. Now my only worry is that my groom won't show up. I've been at my mum's cottage all week planning, and we've barely had a chance to speak."

Jessica laughed. "That's how it's supposed to be before the wedding. This way, you're pining to see each other on the big day. And don't worry, when I drove him here from London yesterday, the wedding was all he could talk about. He'll make it to the venue on time."

It was so sweet to witness these two having each other's backs. I could imagine Gina and I being like this, planning each other's weddings and bossing each other about like sisters.

Sensing an opportunity for some subtle probing about the village, I turned to Lauren and said, "Jessica says you grew up in Broomewode?"

She replied yes but that she'd moved away at eighteen for university and finally relocated to London for work. "I met Ryan, that's my fiancé, because he was the best man when Jessica and her husband, Joe, got married. I was Jessica's maid of honor, of course. Ryan was great. Handsome and funny. We really hit it off when we decorated the honeymoon suite with rose petals together. After the wedding, Jessica set us up on our first date." They exchanged glances and laughed, and I sensed a story there. "And the rest, as they say, is history."

"I can't believe that tomorrow you'll be married," Jessica said, her eyes filling with tears. "How did we get to be actual grownups? I remember when we used to play weddings in primary school."

"Don't you well up." Lauren laughed. "You'll set me off. And there's too much work to be done. Besides, I don't want swollen eyes on my wedding day. We can be sentimental tomorrow. After the photos are done."

Jessica pulled herself together and went to find the two other bridesmaids, Kaitlyn and Kelly. Lauren explained that all the bridesmaids went to secondary school together. Kaitlyn and Kelly were identical twins and inseparable.

I was about to excuse myself and go back to the inn lunch when I saw Edward, the gardener, staggering in under the weight of a giant orange tree.

I rushed over to open the door wider. "Hello again," I said. "I saw you mowing the lawn earlier."

He set the tree down and wiped the soil from his hands on his green gardening uniform. I noticed that he'd caught the sun this week and his nose and forehead were a bit sunburned. "Yeah. There's a lot of lawn. I've still got all the raking to do myself because a couple of the lads have been called down to pretty up the area around the baking tent." He straightened as though his back hurt him. "Had to break off to move trees about," he said, shaking his head at the tree. "Almost broke me back hefting this thing about. Apparently the plants here already don't have enough oranges." He raised an eyebrow before lowering his voice to a whisper. "Is the bride one of them Bridezillas you hear about?"

I shook my head and said that it was the matron of honor he should watch out for—she was the very epitome of high maintenance.

"Gotcha," he said, looking about. "Is that the bride?" He pointed to where Lauren was hanging up a string of fairy lights. "I'll let her know the extra-orangery-orange tree is here."

I realized I was still holding the flowers. I guessed I'd have to find that vase myself.

I found a water jug on a trestle table at the front and put the posy in for a nice drink.

When I returned, Edward and Lauren were giggling like

schoolchildren in the corner. I asked them what was so funny, but that just caused them to double up in fits of laughter.

Lauren wiped a tear from her eye and tried to catch her breath. "This one's a live one," she said, pointing at Edward. "I haven't had a belly giggle like that in ages. Planning a wedding is seriously stressful."

I hadn't noticed Edward being particularly funny before. More serious and reflective, if anything. Oh well. Jessica was calling for Lauren, and she excused herself.

Edward's eyes followed Lauren as she headed out of the Orangery to where Jessica was brandishing ribbon by the rows of chairs for tomorrow's guests.

"You should close that mouth before anyone else sees you gawping at the bride. You do know she's getting married tomorrow, right?" I teased.

He shook his head. "The good ones are always taken before I get there."

Jessica stuck her head round the door. "Poppy, come meet the other bridesmaids. They're fans too."

Oh man, was I ever going to get out of here? I had Bundt cake recipes to go over—not to mention a ravenous appetite to satisfy. I seriously needed some lunch. Maybe a roast beef baguette with horseradish. Some salad on the side to be good.

"Come along," Jessica insisted.

I smiled tightly and allowed myself to be led outside.

Kaitlyn and Kelly were indeed the spitting images of each other: petite frames, intense wide, blue eyes set close together, long, straight noses, and jet-black hair cut into a sleek, swaying bob for one sister, whereas the other had hair down to her waist. They smiled at me simultaneously, flashing neat rows of pearly-white teeth.

The bridesmaids asked after the cake, and I told them about its sumptuous buttercream, the combination of bright, uplifting lemon and creamy, fruity coconut. I was proud. Even to my ears, the cake sounded delicious, and I was glad I'd managed to do a good job for these sweet women.

Jessica handed me a small bag with lengths of ribbon for my cake. She really was well-organized.

"And are you married, Poppy?" Kaitlyn asked. "We're hoping to find our perfect matches at the wedding—like how Lauren and Ryan met at Jessica's wedding."

"No. Not yet." Not only was I not married, I wasn't likely to ever be a wife unless I could find a man who accepted that I was a witch who talked to ghosts. Single forever then.

Kelly grabbed my hand. "Come on, you can join us in the ritual."

Ritual? Had I stumbled on a wedding party of witches? I must have looked alarmed because Kelly giggled and said, "It's a Broomewode tradition—Lauren told us all about it."

Jessica grinned. "Let them show you. I can't take part, as I'm already married. I'm going to space out these chairs."

I let myself be dragged back to the reception room. Kaitlyn rushed over to the corner, where a small stone statue of Cupid presided on an elaborately chiseled pedestal.

"Isn't he cute?" Kaitlyn said fondly, patting the statue's head. I had to agree. The chubby cherub had been carved from smooth, white stone and had a sweet, pouting mouth and a head of swirling curls. Intricate, feathered wings sprung out from his back, and he was carrying a bow and arrow.

"First of all, close your eyes and picture the kind of man you want to marry," Kelly commanded. "How he looks, what he does, the kind of father he'll be."

At that last comment, my eyes flicked back open. The only thing I could imagine was a cake in the oven, not a bun in the oven.

"Close your eyes, Poppy," Kaitlyn said. "You've got to concentrate if you want this to work."

Hmm. I wasn't so sure I did want this to work. I tried to imagine my dream man, but I had no idea who that might be or what he might look like. As if there was room for romance in my busy schedule, what with the baking show, being a witch, and searching for my birth parents.

"Now focus on your heart," Kelly continued. "Imagine it as a glowing mass of energy, shining a light out into the universe, seeking out your dream man."

Oh my. These girls were really something.

"You doing it?" Kaitlyn asked.

"Mmhm," I murmured. I couldn't see his face but I imagined the feel of strong arms around me, felt the warmth of loving and being loved by a man who would want me even though I was so different from most women.

And while I envisioned this man, she said these words:

> While the heart's eye is blind
> Love sees from soul to soul
> Cupid, bring this love to bind
> Two perfect halves into a whole

"Open your eyes. Now rub his belly for good luck, like a Buddha's," Kelly commanded.

I laughed and obeyed her command. She was almost as bossy as Jessica. Also hearing her recite the old rhyme was like hearing a spell cast. Maybe I wasn't so different from other women after all. These bridesmaids were taking part in the ancient ritual of marriage and reciting love spells. I could imagine joining hands with them under the moon some night and greeting them as sisters.

"And keep thinking loving thoughts as you do it," Kaitlyn added.

It was nice to fantasize about romance for a change instead of a bowl full of glossy buttercream.

"Okay, all done," I said. "How soon till my dream man falls in love with me?"

"Oh, any day now," Kaitlyn said, laughing. She pulled a piece of purple ribbon from her back pocket and tied it in a bow around Cupid's neck. "Bring the best men for us," she whispered. Then she laughed. "Maybe we'll find our partners this evening at the wedding rehearsal."

I chuckled. These girls were so lovely. I was glad to have been brought into their world—even if it was just for a day.

Jessica's voice suddenly boomed from outside, and Kaitlyn and Kelly straightened and shot each other desperate looks. "Back to the grind," Kaitlyn said. "If I ever get married, Jessica will be the last to know. See you later, Poppy."

I waved them off and turned back to face the cupid. "Could a sweet thing like you really make me lucky in love?" I asked.

The angelic face stared back at me with his wide, unblinking eyes. And then I couldn't help myself. I began to wonder if I could move something this big just by concentrating. I stole a quick look around the room, but everyone was outside doing Jessica's bidding with the chairs.

I turned back and then tried to summon the same focus I'd used earlier to lift the rose from the vase. I narrowed my eyes and put all my concentration to the sensation of channeling my energy into the cupid. A fizzing feeling began to bubble up in my belly. *That's it, that's it,* I thought, trying to encourage whatever magic forces were at play to push themselves that little bit further. But no luck. Cupid stood firm on his pedestal. *Don't give up, Pops,* I imagined Gerry cheering me on. I tried again, this time using my index finger as though it were a magic wand. Time and space seemed to recede. There was only me and Cupid. I heard my breathing, felt my power coming from some ancient source and channeling through me. Before my eyes, the cupid lifted up into the air, hovered for a split second and then dropped back to its pedestal.

Cool! I couldn't believe I'd done it. I'd moved not only a single rose but a heavy stone statue. That was wild. I was seriously impressed with my new talent. If I kept going at this rate, who knew what I could eventually end up lifting? A human being? A car? I mean, I was aiming for superwoman status here.

"Poppy?"

I felt the blood draining from my face and my heart beat wildly. Had I just been busted? I stood frozen to the spot.

"Poppy?"

I turned round slowly, expecting the worst. But to my utter joy, Susan Bentley's smiling face greeted me. And by the looks of it, she'd missed my brief foray into the world of levitating cupids.

Susan was wearing an olive-green smock dress, and her reddish cropped curls had been recently cut. The streaks of gray at her temples were more pronounced and lent her features a more distinguished look. I complimented her dress. Susan had definitely been making an effort with her appearance lately.

"Thank you," Susan said, touching the folds of her dress a little self-consciously. "I'm making an effort to dress every day, eat well and get out more." She shook her head. She hadn't been widowed very long, and I could imagine how important those routines were to her. She glanced around. "I hear you made the wedding cake. How lovely."

Did nothing stay secret in this village? Except the story of my birth parents.

I told her all about my adventures with the Bundt cake this week and how I'd managed to squeeze in a lemon and coconut wedding cake, too.

Susan listened wide-eyed and then chuckled that throaty laugh of hers. "Never not doing a million things at once, Poppy. Make sure you can still keep your head in the competition. You're going to need a stellar weekend of baking to get back on track."

Hmm. Seemed everyone in Broomewode knew I'd slipped last week too. And did they *all* have to remind me? Time for some deflection. I pointed at the large wicker basket in Susan's arms. "Did you get roped in too?"

"Wedding favors," she said, smiling proudly. "Look." She pulled back the length of checked fabric covering the top of the basket, and I peered inside. Little pots of honey were lined up in neat rows, each tied with a thin purple bow. I guessed Jessica had convinced everyone in the village to help with the wedding arrangements.

"These are so pretty," I exclaimed. I picked up a pot. *Lauren and Ryan,* the handwritten label said, and *"May your lives together bee sweet."* And the wedding date in small letters beneath. "They must have taken you ages."

"Oh, yes, but it was worth it. I wasn't sure about the slogan, but Jessica insisted."

"She's very determined." Just then I heard a familiar bark. "Is that?" I asked.

"Sly's outside, with his red ball, of course. I'm sure he'll be delighted to see you." She put her basket down on the nearest table and began to take out the wedding favors, only to be called by Jessica, who insisted on seeing the finished product. With a quick eye roll, she picked up two of the jars and headed out to the veranda. Sly barked again, and I turned round to bid the cupid farewell, but the stone pedestal was empty. Cupid wasn't there.

"What the?" I said aloud. "Where did you go?"

I spun round in a circle, and there was the statue, looking all innocent next to an orange tree.

"How did you get there? I didn't try to move you again." Maybe I hadn't got such a great grip on my new powers. I walked over and picked up the statue (in the conventional way, with my arms) and returned it to its pedestal.

"Now stay," I admonished.

I turned and made to leave, but suddenly, there was the statue, blocking my exit route.

I had to laugh. "You cheeky cherub."

I looked around the room. No one was here. Could this be Gerry's doing? He'd managed to move items around. Had he figured out how to float beyond the tent and inn and poltergeist elsewhere?

"Is that you, Gerry? Show yourself!"

Nothing.

I picked up the cupid and set him down in his rightful place. "Stay there," I commanded. I had enough to contend with this weekend without a wandering statue following me about.

I found Sly outside, red ball in his mouth, tail wagging furiously.

"Hello, boy," I called. "I've missed you."

He came bounding over, and I ruffled his thick black and white fur. The ball dropped at my feet. "Well, that didn't take long." I laughed, obliging him by hurling the ball. I had succumbed to the notion that today was simply about doing other people's—and dog's—bidding.

But as I straightened, I saw Sly pick up speed and follow the ball's trajectory right into the pretty stream. Oh, dear. I hoped Susan wouldn't mind a soggy Sly.

I walked toward the water. Sly splashed about, searching for his ball. He let out a little woof of happiness when he spied it, then grabbed the wet ball in his jaws and bounded out, his gorgeous fur slicked to his body.

"Don't even think about it," I said, watching as Sly prepared to shake himself dry. He lifted a paw. It was covered in blades of grass.

"Oh no," I said. "The gardener just mowed the lawns, and now you've got half the grass on you."

Sly shook his body, and water and blades of grass went flying. I stepped back, laughing. He finished his dry-off and then dropped his ball back at my feet. "Just one more throw,"

I warned him, "And then I have to get back to work. My real work. I've got cookbooks waiting to be read and a long weekend of baking ahead of me."

And it was imperative that I leave Cupid and the brides behind and get to work.

CHAPTER 5

I left Lauren and the bridesmaids to finish the decorating so they could get ready for the wedding rehearsal and wished them luck. My stomach was growling, so I told Susan I was heading back to the inn. She said she'd join me for lunch once she'd finished setting out the wedding favors. I was about to offer to help her put them out when Jessica came in looking very officious. She had a wooden ruler in her hand. When she started telling Susan exactly how many inches from the edge of the table to place the pots and began to demonstrate exactly how she wanted them, I decided I'd only be in the way.

Abandoning poor Susan to her fate—no doubt she'd get her hand slapped with that ruler if she put one honey pot an inch out of place—I set off toward the pub, and lunch, with a spring in my step, grateful to be involved in this happy wedding with such bubbly girls, feeling that I'd come up with a cake that would make the bride proud. Now for getting my head back into the competition. I didn't need anyone else reminding me I had my work cut out.

But as I walked, I had the distinct sensation of being watched. Had the cupid followed me out of the Orangery? I spun round. Nothing there. And then, in a tree, I saw a hawk. He was perched on a low branch, staring at me. I looked back at him, admiring his plume, the scattering of white on his rich brown body, the cinnamon-red of his tail. His beak was curved and sharp, his eyes even sharper. My immediate thought was that he was a hunter and my poor familiar was still barely more than a kitten.

I raced back to the inn and found Gateau happily playing in the flowerbeds. "I'm going to have to keep a closer eye on you," I said, scooping her up into my arms. She gave me a look, as if to say, *Try it.* I supposed she had her own powers that were probably stronger than that hawk's. I hoped so.

She butted my arm with her head.

"I'm going to take that as a yes."

Gateau and I walked into the pub and pulled up a seat at the bar, where Eve was pouring a gin and tonic. It looked tempting, but (of course) I had to keep my eyes on the prize. No refreshing alcoholic beverages until I'd baked my way back into the show's Top Three.

I ordered a fresh orange juice from Eve and debated whether to satisfy my craving for a roast beef baguette or try the special. "It's pesto, chargrilled vegetables and creamy mozzarella from the deli in the village," Eve prompted.

"Sold," I said. "Any chance of something for Gateau here?"

Eve said she'd go see what treats they had in the kitchen. "I know this kitty has expensive taste."

Eve returned with my baguette. It was warm and crusty,

the mozzarella just beginning to melt into the chargrilled vegetables. Perfect.

"And I haven't forgotten you, either," she said to Gateau, setting down two generous slices of roast chicken.

"But have you forgotten me?" I jumped, hearing the voice so close to me.

It was Gerry. Oh man, I so did not need to be seen talking to thin air right now. I scowled at Gerry and raised one eyebrow in warning. Of course, he took no notice and turned a somersault in the air, righting himself and then hovering over the barstool next to me. Eve turned to serve some customers, and in a whisper, I said, "Gerry, what have I told you? Don't try to chat with me in public."

"Sorry, Pops, just wanted to make you laugh. You looked so serious."

At that, I felt bad. Poor Gerry must be so bored.

"I appreciate it, but you nearly gave me a heart attack with your hijinks earlier."

Gerry raised his palms in defense. "What you talking 'bout?"

"Poltergeist-ing that cupid statue in the Orangery so that it followed me around," I whispered. "If you were trying to remind me how single I am, you needn't have bothered. The entire bridal party managed to make me feel like the forever singleton without you."

"The Orangery? I might be able to move objects now, but I swear I can still only travel between here and the tent." He shook his head sorrowfully, a morose expression on his face. "I'm trapped." Gerry looked so genuinely baffled that I began to wonder whether the whole incident had really happened.

Could I add hallucinations to my growing list of personality traits? I took another bite of my crusty baguette.

Luckily Gerry's somber mood didn't last long. He spotted a couple in the penthouse suite that he'd been haunting making their way to a corner table and went to terrorize them further.

Eve returned and started chatting about the wedding. It seemed that Jessica had roped other Broomewode villagers into the preparations. Everyone was buzzed about tomorrow's nuptials, and many of the guests were booked into the inn.

"It's a full house this weekend. We're going to be rushed off our feet. Good for business, though." She pointed at a table of men who looked to be in their twenties, except for one who was graying at the temples and was probably in his early fifties. "They're part of the wedding party. The one in the middle is Ryan, the groom, and the older gentleman next to him is his dad, Harry."

I pivoted on my stool and watched the group of laughing men, who were busy finishing off their drinks. The groom was just as handsome as I'd imagined—a perfect match for Lauren's natural beauty. Like the bride, he had blond hair, though his was a shade darker and cropped closely to his head, the sides shorn close to the skin. He was wearing a loose white linen shirt with a granddaddy collar—very London trendy. The other two young men were brunette, similarly dressed in trendy shirts and indigo jeans. They had the easy air of a group of friends who'd known each other for years. I wondered which one was Jessica's husband. The groom looked at his watch and gasped. He stood and said, "Come on, you lot. We've got the wedding rehearsal." With

NANCY WARREN

the last sip downed, the men stood and walked past the bar. Eve raised her hand and wished them well for their rehearsal.

The older gentleman's face crinkled into a wide grin, and he broke away from the group. "That's the father of the groom," Eve said softly. "He may be old, but he's the one to watch out for." And then she could say no more for he was in front of us.

Up close, I could see the similarities between him and his son. They were both classically handsome: sparkling blue eyes set close to a Roman nose, high cheekbones and a strong jaw, but where Ryan was fair, his dad had dark brown hair shot through with gray.

"Don't worry, Eve," he said, "I'll be back before you know it. Maybe tonight is the night you'll join me for a nightcap?"

"I'll certainly give the proposal some thought." Eve laughed good-naturedly.

"I bet you're a scotch gal." He paused, waiting for an answer. "Am I right?"

"Of course you're right. You've not been here twenty-four hours, but I've already seen you're as good as me at predicting people's poison."

Harry demurely bowed his head and then shot me a grin. "And perhaps your pretty friend might join us, as well."

"That pretty friend has a name: It's Poppy."

"A pretty name for a pretty lady." He stepped forward and offered his hand, and as I reached out to shake it, he took my palm and kissed it. I giggled. Although his moves were old-fashioned, coming from such a suave character, they felt debonair, and he had such charm that what would be creepy in most old guys seemed sweet and harmless coming from him.

"She also happens to be the wonderful baker who stepped in last-minute to bake Lauren and Ryan's cake."

He raised two thick, dark eyebrows. "Ah, Poppy, of course —you're our heroine. I've heard all about you. My son tells me that you're on *The Great British Baking Contest.* In my head, I'd pictured a kindly grandmother type with half-moon glasses and a floral apron—not a gorgeous thing like you. It's an honor to meet you."

I shook my head. A baking heroine. Honestly.

"Now be gone with you, Harry," Eve admonished. "The father of the groom can't be late."

"Very true, very true," he said. "I am the life and soul of the party. I don't know what those young fools would do without me." He performed a mock bow and then caught up with the rest of the men who were waiting by the door.

"If they didn't look so alike, I wouldn't have believed that silver-tongued fox was Ryan's dad. He doesn't look old enough."

Eve couldn't seem to take her eyes off the older man— Harry certainly seemed to have an effect on women. "Handsome and a rogue to boot," she said. "You should have seen him at dinner last night, holding court at the table, telling stories and buying rounds of tequila. He's incorrigible. But I can't help going all soft when he smiles at me."

I grinned. "And is there a Mrs. Incorrigible?"

Eve's expression became solemn. "Sadly, he's a widower."

"Ah, I see." I gave Eve a knowing look. Would it be too much to add matchmaker as another string to my bow? I might not have any luck with love myself, but after rubbing Cheeky Cupid's belly today, perhaps I could summon up some good romantic fortune for my fellow witches.

"I can read you like a spellbook, Poppy Wilkinson," Eve said, wagging a finger at me. "And let me just stop those thoughts right there. You've enough on your plate without trying to set me up. Now be a good little witch and finish up your sandwich before it goes stone cold."

I obeyed Eve's command—although no one ever had to tell me twice to finish a meal—and was savoring the last morsel when Susan Bentley waved at me and came over to join us.

I pulled out the barstool next to me. Susan sat down with a sigh, massaging her temples with her fingertips. "Oof, that bridal party has exhausted me. I thought I'd never get out of there. The matron of honor had me measuring exactly where to put each pot of honey. That woman's a nightmare. I answered so many questions about my honey. The breed of bees, the size of the hives, the specific flavor profile. I mean, it's nice that someone takes an interest, but really the little pots are just adorable wedding favors. I don't think anyone is going to quiz the bride about honey." She shook her head.

I felt my heart sink. What would happen to me tomorrow when the Broomewode Hall catering team delivered my cake and I added the final decorations?

Eve's response was to pour Susan a glass of rosé.

"How did you know?" Susan grinned, taking a long drink.

"And I bet the Spanish Inquisition came from Jessica, not Lauren, the actual bride," I said.

"How did *you* know?" Susan laughed. "The sisterhood is in sync."

I smiled at Susan and Eve. I really was so lucky to have found my coven. And now it was time to take advantage of their experience and ask for some advice. I lowered my voice until it was a barely audible whisper and explained that I'd discovered today that I could move objects with my thoughts alone.

"You mean you have telekinesis," Susan said, seemingly not surprised in the slightest.

"Telekinesis?" That sounded like an angry dry skin condition to my ears.

Susan laughed. "It's the proper term for moving objects by mental power alone. I knew that some witches had this gift but none that I know."

"Same," Eve said. "It's pretty advanced, Poppy. Especially for a witch who's only just discovered her powers."

I told them both about moving the rose stem and then about the Cupid statue, the silly ritual with the bridesmaids and how I'd rubbed his belly. "Then the statue started following me around the Orangery even though I wasn't trying to move it anymore."

"Perhaps you've tied your energy to the cupid statue by touching it?" Eve suggested.

My energy? I hoped not. I was going to need every ounce of energy to get through the next few days, thanks very much. And the last thing I needed was a marble cupid drifting into view when I was baking on camera. That would be memorable but for all the wrong reasons.

A young man came up to the bar, and Eve moved away to pour him a pint of ale.

"Sounds like you used a little too much focus with that cupid, Poppy," Susan said, suddenly looking serious.

Well, *too* much focus was something I hadn't been accused of lately. Usually it was all *Get your head back in the game, Pops,* or *Bake harder!*

Susan lowered her voice another notch and tucked a stray curl behind her ear. "You have to be very careful with how you use your powers. You're still new at all of this, and you've much to learn about your abilities."

I nodded sincerely. Didn't I know it.

I PASSED the rest of the afternoon back in my room, studying recipes, memorizing the method so I'd be smooth when caught on camera and asked to describe my process. I could heed Susan's words when it came to witchcraft, but I couldn't rest on my laurels when it came to European Bakes week. Gateau stayed by my side, snoozing and letting out little snores of cattish contentment, no doubt dreaming of tuna treats and lording over the butterfly kingdom.

Luckily, Gerry had taken the hint earlier, and I was left in ghost-less peace. In fact, I'd been studying for so long, I'd barely noticed the sky change from blue to a gorgeous hue of burnt orange until the sun had become just a burning round ball on the horizon. Perhaps I wouldn't have noticed time passing at all, had it not been for a series of growls emanating from my stomach. I checked my watch and was surprised to find it was already seven-thirty p.m. Dinner was calling. There was nothing for it but to head back downstairs, and since it was now evening, I was going to treat myself to a large gin and tonic and watch the rest of the sunset.

The other contestants weren't due to arrive until tomorrow, so it would be a good chance for me to try and speak to some of the locals without arousing any suspicions. The more info I could gather about the community, the better, especially now that Katie had confirmed Valerie had left Broomewode pregnant. It was all the confirmation I needed that I knew who my birth mother was. Well, I had a first name and some gossip to go on. Someone somewhere must know more about Valerie.

But when I got downstairs, the pub was busy, and a party atmosphere prevailed. I looked around in dismay, scanning the room for a spare seat. But the bridal party had returned from their rehearsal and had clearly now moved on to rehearsing for tomorrow's reception. I could barely hear myself think over the guffaws and clinking glasses. Even so, the unmistakable scent of steak and ale pie was in the air, and I could see that it was on the specials board for the evening. I had to get an order in before the last pie was snapped up. Eve caught my eye and motioned me over to the bar.

"It's absolute carnage in here tonight with that wedding party," she said, sounding exhausted. Her long braid had loosened, and a few gray threads framed her face, her cheeks pink and glistening. Poor Eve. She was on a double shift today. I didn't know where she found the stamina.

"I wish I could help you," I said, "but my strengths lie more on the spatula side of things. I don't know the first thing about pulling a pint."

"I wouldn't let you near these pipes." Eve grinned. "This pub is ancient, and it needs a steady, knowledgeable hand— not a telekinetic witch."

Well, that told me.

A couple left their barstools, and Eve told me to grab one while I could. "Time yet for that gin and tonic?" she asked.

It was like she could read my mind.

I accepted the glass from Eve with pleasure, listening to

the ice cubes crackle, watching the lime wedge float on its bubbly surface. I took a long sip and—ahh—the events of the day began to slip away. I turned to examine the specials board and watched as the groom's party continued their raucous celebrations. They were a high-spirited bunch. But as long as there were no actual spirits, then I could deal with it. Besides, it was fun to feel part of the celebration.

I spotted the groom and his dad and some of the young men he'd been sitting with earlier. No sign of the twins or Jessica yet, and I guessed that Lauren would spend her final single evening at her mum's, away from her future husband, as tradition dictated. And if tradition dictated that the groom also drank too much before the wedding night, then Ryan's dad, Harry, was behind it with aplomb. I could hear his insistence for a round of shots from where I was sitting. I checked my watch. Eight p.m. already. Oh, dear.

"Don't be soft, lads. Time for shots," Harry called out again.

Ryan shook his head. "Dad, let's slow down, shall we?"

"This is your last night of freedom, my son, and we shall send you off with a bang." Harry stood and made his way over to the bar. He stopped and turned back to the table. "After all, you only get married once." He laughed loudly. "We hope."

I caught Eve's eye. "Play it cool," I whispered, grinning.

Harry arrived and said, "Eve, you're looking gorgeous tonight. And Poppy. You're a vision for sore eyes." He ordered twelve shots of tequila. Eve rolled her eyes at him, but I could see she was pleased by the attention and went to fetch more shot glasses from the back. Harry inquired about my afternoon and then asked me to join the bridal party for a tequila-style toast. I thanked him but shook my head. I couldn't let myself get distracted this evening. I was here for a quick supper, maybe a bit of chatting up anyone who might have known Valerie, and then it was an early night. But Harry wouldn't take no for an answer. He appealed to Eve, who was busy pouring dangerously large shots of tequila into a row of glasses.

"Don't you agree that after all Poppy's hard work on the wedding cake, she should at least let me show my appreciation with a little tipple?"

Eve raised a brow but stayed silent. *Thanks, Eve. Way to come to my defense.*

Harry's cheeky blue eyes glittered. "Go on, pour another shot for Poppy here," he said to Eve.

I held up my hands. "Okay, okay. One drink. But *not* a tequila."

Harry grinned. "Eve, darling, would you be so kind as to add a gin and tonic to my tab?" Harry picked up the tray of shots and motioned for me to follow with my drink.

Just a quick hello to the group and then I'd make my excuses, I promised myself as Eve poured me a fresh gin and tonic.

The wedding party was squeezed around the largest table in the pub. One side was taken up with a long bench, the other crammed with chairs and stools. A candelabra with red tapered candles took center stage. An army of empty glasses surrounded it. Harry pulled out a chair and gestured for me to sit. He introduced me as, "This gorgeous young thing who made your wedding cake is Poppy."

They all greeted me with friendly comments. Like the

bridesmaids I'd met earlier, the men of the wedding party seemed like a lovely bunch.

"Here's the man of the hour," Harry said, sounding proud. "This is my son, Ryan."

"I can tell." I laughed. "The resemblance between you two is striking."

"He got my looks and his mother's brains, lucky for him."

"I couldn't possibly comment," I teased back.

Ryan thanked me for stepping in last minute to help with the cake. "Lauren was so happy, she nearly cried," he told me. Up close, he had a kind face, and although his cheekbones were more chiseled than his father's, there was something softer about him, too. He was wearing a white linen shirt, and a small silver chain glinted between the open buttons.

Spirits were high, and I tried to remember everyone's name. It was a real pleasure to be around people who were set on having a good time. No dramas. No baking pressure. No ghostly business. Just people celebrating true love. It was hard not to absorb their enthusiasm.

Harry handed out the shots and a bowl of lime wedges. He stood. "I'd like to make a toast to my son and future daughter-in-law—who, no doubt, is being far more sensible than us right now and probably has her hair in curlers and her feet up in front of the TV."

Everyone laughed.

"She's onto something, that fiancée of mine," Ryan said softly to me. "I'm going to need a gallon of water before bed tonight. My dad turns everything into an all-night party. He's worse than any of my mates." He spoke with a kind of irritated affection.

Harry raised his glass. "To Ryan and Lauren, may they

have a long and happy future together—with their hair in curlers and watching TV."

There was more laughter, and the group knocked back their tequila shots. A lot of coughing ensued. I took a demure sip of my gin and tonic.

"So tell me, pretty Poppy," Harry said, "are you spoken for? There's many a fine young man at the table here who could use a beautiful woman who can bake."

Oh dear, was it going to be like this all weekend? Strangers trying to set me up or dragging me into their love-superstitions? It was worse than being told how to make the perfect scone over and over again.

I laughed and tried to push the question away.

"How about Julius?" He pointed at the man sitting to the left of Ryan. He had a head of thick black curls, short at the sides and longer on the top so that a few strands fell over his forehead. His eyes were dark and set either side of an elegant, long nose. He was wearing a navy shirt, the top two buttons left open so that a few chest hairs were visible. There was a trace of dark stubble, too, lending his features a contoured look. He was talking with some intensity to Ryan, in a whisper so low I couldn't quite make out the words.

Harry prodded me. "One of Ryan's oldest friends, twenty-nine, single for a year after a three-year relationship, works in engineering—on RAF planes, I believe—so good with his hands." Harry paused and chuckled, evidently pleased with himself.

What was this? A dating show?

"Thanks for the stats, Harry," I said. "But I'm quite content to be on my own at the moment."

I could see that Harry was about to protest, but luckily a

waitress walked by and Harry stopped her to ask for another round of shots. A collective groan went up from the table. "How is the oldest one here getting the rest of us so tipsy?" a pretty woman said.

I turned my attention back to Ryan and Julius, but it seemed their conversation had turned intense. And private.

Ryan looked worried and was shaking his head. "Look, mate, I understand the timing's tricky. But what can I do?"

Julius brushed his curls from his forehead. His voice was urgent. "I just need a few more weeks. That's all."

"I don't have that long. We have a viewing booked for a week after the wedding, Julius. If she falls in love with the house she'll expect me to make an offer." Ryan looked worried.

The groomsman looked sick.

Julius must have felt eyes on him because he suddenly turned from Ryan and looked back toward the group. I fixed my gaze on my gin and tonic, pretending to be mesmerized by its bubbles. Whatever those two were talking about, it sounded serious. But for now, Ryan was all smiles again, and he raised his beer glass to me.

I was wondering whether I'd played the part of gracious cake-maker for long enough and could politely excuse myself when another guy approached the table. He had the same shade of blond hair as Lauren—the same snub nose, too, and judging by his age, looked to be her older brother. Unlike the rest of the wedding group, he was wearing a casual white T-shirt and jeans. And he wasn't wearing a smile. Instead, his broad forehead was creased into a frown, and he seemed to be sweating. Did he not get the memo? Even if it was the day before the big event, weddings were supposed to be about fun and celebration.

Harry stood and clapped the man on the back. "George, old boy," he said. "Let me get you a drink. It's a vodka tonic, as I recall?" He really had mastered the convivial father-of-the-groom part.

But George did not share my admiration. He shook off Harry's hand and slumped onto a stool, immediately pulling out his phone and tapping away at the screen. A woman sat down next to him, and from the tender way she kissed his forehead, I assumed it was his wife. He smiled at her, and she mouthed something to him that I couldn't quite catch.

I was about to take off when a girl on my other side introduced herself to me as Jessica's little sister. I listened as she told me about her apprenticeship at a London hairdresser's. Was I ever going to be able to leave to go and study some more? I checked myself. Did I really want to be the only twenty-five-year-old in the world who desperately tried to leave a pub in order to get back to her books?

Harry returned with George's drink, but the younger man didn't even acknowledge him as he carefully set it down on the crowded table. He put a glass of red wine in front of the woman, and she barely gave a nod. How rude. Harry didn't appear to be fazed, however, and pulled up a chair. "Now that my son's marrying your sister, you'll be my other son. And you, my daughter-in-law."

Harry gave George a hearty smile, and I have to admit, my stomach flipped a bit. Not because I was sweet on Harry (that was all Eve's terrain) but because of how welcoming he was, inviting people into the fold, telling George he was a son to him now. I wished someone would welcome me into their family. I thought of how many times I'd been thwarted trying to find out more about Valerie, and I had a moment where I wished I was marrying Ryan and being so heartily welcomed by Harry.

George's head flashed up. It was obvious he was about to say something cutting to Harry but then thought better of it. He murmured "cheers" instead and picked up his drink, clinking his glass with his wife's.

Harry turned his focus back to me and Jessica's sister, and they chatted about tomorrow's breakfast arrangements. Now that I could relate to—I loved to plan my next meal before my current one had even finished. But I was intrigued by George. Something was clearly on his mind.

George was still tapping on his phone, but when Ryan returned from the bathroom, he quickly put it down. I tuned out of the omelet versus scrambled egg debate and trained my attention on the men.

George rose and confronted Ryan before he could sit down again. "I love my sister, and I've got my eye on you. I've heard the rumors. If I find out you've hurt her, I'll––"

Ryan looked mortified. But before George could finish, Harry turned to face him, patting him on the shoulder. "No doubt Ryan was sowing his wild oats. All that will be behind him now. Your sister's a beaut. No man would turn his back on her."

Wowzers. Had Ryan cheated on Lauren? She was such a mega babe and a sweetheart to boot. What more could a man want? Jessica had given me the impression that those two were love's young dream. A perfect match. What was up with the brother?

George's face was red, and he glared at his future brother-in-law in a way that did not bode well for future family events, then downed the rest of his drink and left. His wife gazed after him but, interestingly, didn't follow. Maybe she didn't want to get an earful. I didn't blame her. George looked to me like he'd had too much to drink and was one of those guys who brooded over injustices, real and imagined, when he'd been drinking.

I used his exit as a good excuse for mine and thanked Harry for the drink. I was about to head back to the bar to order that steak and ale pie when Jessica walked in. Oh, man. Was I about to get bombarded with a thousand cake queries? But Jessica didn't seem to notice me. She walked straight past, like she was on a mission—no doubt to tell the wedding party they were doing their celebrations all wrong. I watched as she went to greet everyone, admiring her gorgeous outfit. She'd changed out of her earlier dress and into a cream silk two-piece: a beautifully cut camisole tucked into a pair of wide-legged silk trousers. The pale color set off her long, dark hair perfectly.

"Everything's ready for the big day," I heard her report, though no one looked to be listening.

I left them to it and decided against the pie, ordering instead the grilled plaice special with Eve at the bar. The pub was still seriously bustling, and she was rushed off her feet. I sank into the barstool and took the final sip of my drink. I had a long weekend ahead of me, and if I could just get through tomorrow morning, putting the final touches to the wedding cake, then all of my attention and energy could be poured into the baking show. And if I happened to chat with some of the Broomewode staff and ask them about a woman named Valerie, well then, all the better.

Lauren and Jessica were about my age, so chances were their mothers might have known Valerie if they'd been locals too. A glance around the pub told me that this was the social hub of the village. I hoped I'd have a chance to chat to the parents at the reception in the hope that someone had known the woman I thought of as my birth mother.

My fish arrived, and I tucked straight in. It was perfectly grilled, soft and flaky on the inside and covered in a brown butter sauce with capers. I sliced a new potato in half and sighed happily.

But my little moment of fish heaven was interrupted by Harry's booming voice. "Lord Winford," he called out. "What a pleasure. Come and join us for a drink."

I turned round to see Benedict and a man I didn't recognize. Maybe Benedict did have friends after all.

Benedict smiled and went to join them, and more cries of "Lord Winford!" went up from the group. They addressed him by his title with such enthusiasm. Surely that had to be totally embarrassing? But it appeared he was taking it all in good spirits, chatting and laughing away.

I finished up my dinner and told Eve that I was heading upstairs to hunker down to my cookbooks. She kissed my cheek and wished me a restful evening. I was about to get up when I felt a strong hand on my shoulder.

I turned. Benedict's hair was shorter than the last time I saw him, and it made him look quite dapper, as the British would say. "Ah, Lord Winford," I greeted him as they had done, "slumming it with the village folks tonight?"

He grinned. "If using my title and shaking a few hands helps save this estate, I'll do it. All part of the service."

I was surprised Benedict took my teasing so gracefully.

Maybe he really *had* grown a sense of humor while I'd been away this week.

He gestured to my empty glass. "Will you have another?" Like he was a normal guy chatting up a woman at the pub.

I was actually tempted, then Harry's voice boomed, "Now, Lord Winford, you must tell us about this naughty ancestor of yours we've been hearing about. The one who built the Orangery."

Benedict's eye roll was so subtle, only I could see it. I thanked him for the drink offer but told him I had to rest up for the morning. "Besides, you've got to tell stories about your naughty ancestors."

"They weren't that naughty," he said, but I only laughed and headed out.

CHAPTER 6

*B*ack upstairs, I was grateful to escape the raucous wedding party and all of its insider politics. I pulled the cord of the lampshade, and the room was cast in a warm glow. The stack of cookbooks I'd been making my way through earlier was waiting for me on the bedside table, so I kicked off my shoes and collapsed onto the mattress. There was no sign of Gateau. She must have been out prowling, doing her feline thing. I reached for one of my favorite dessert books by a famous French patisserie owner, but it slid away from me as though pulled by an unseen hand.

"Oh no," I whined out loud. "I've got to get my new powers under control." What if I was baking on camera and my Bundt cake started dancing in the air?

A snicker came from behind me. I whipped round. "Gerry!"

"Sorry, Pops. Couldn't resist."

I chucked the book in his direction. Gerry dodged it—despite the fact it would only have gone through him anyway. "Off with you," I said, wagging my finger in the schoolmistress manner. "I've had a long day, and all I want is some quiet time with my recipes."

"You're no fun," Gerry said, pouting. "I'll go and toy with someone else."

He floated through the door.

"And since you're so good at moving things now," I called out, "perhaps you can find a way of knocking from now on. Don't make me ask a third time."

I heard faint diabolical laughter from the corridor.

Gateau scrambled through the window. "Oh, so now you appear," I said. "Do you have an internal ghost-clock or something? I could have really used you as a spirit-deterrent about five minutes ago." She innocently mewed at me and curled up at the bottom of the bed.

I got myself ready for sleep and slipped between the sheets with my beloved cookbook, settling in for a satisfying read about choux pastry.

I was about to nod off when I heard Jessica's booming voice. She must have been given the room next to me. I groaned. I hoped she wasn't going to continue barking orders in her sleep.

Soon enough, a man's voice joined in. Oh great. Her husband, Joe, must have joined her. I guess you'd also have to be loud if you were going to get a word in edgewise being married to Jessica.

Their voices were muffled, but they didn't sound like the happiest couple. No doubt she was telling him off about his shoes not being lined up correctly or his suitcase packed too sloppily.

I concentrated on the recipe in front of me, and the voices soon faded. As did I. I found myself drifting off. Noise or no noise, it had been a long week, and sleep was calling me.

THE CHATTER of blackbirds woke me in the morning. I rubbed my eyes. Sunlight was streaming through the open window. I'd been so tired last night, I'd forgotten to draw the curtains. I carefully maneuvered my legs—Gateau had taken to sleeping directly on top of my feet in the night—but my sweet feline was nowhere to be seen.

I had a quick, reviving shower, pulled on a pair of jeans and a striped blue T-shirt, and headed downstairs. It was already nine a.m., and if I was going to get the cake decorations completed before the ceremony, I'd have to get a move on. I didn't want Taskmaster Jessica breathing down my neck —plus a few more fresh flowers wouldn't go amiss. I could pick some en route to make sure I had plenty to play with. This was my first catering job, after all, and it couldn't be anything short of a roaring success.

I poured a cup of strong black coffee and spread some toast with a thick layer of raspberry jam. The pub was quiet and tidy, but I wondered how late the party had gone last night and how many sore heads there'd be this wedding-day morning. While I enjoyed my coffee, I called over to Broomewode kitchen and asked them to put the wedding cake in place in the Orangery and I'd put the finishing touches on it there.

I was smugly pleased with myself for being well-rested and sober as I strolled out of the inn.

It was a perfect late spring day. The sun coming through

the whitebeam trees dappled the grounds around the inn, and their leaves danced in the gentle breeze. A sparrow hopped across the grass before suddenly flying up, circling a tree and then disappearing from sight. A few clouds moved across the blue sky in that slow, elegant way of theirs, and the air had that pleasant, early-morning freshness to it. What a wonderful day to get married.

The crunch of gravel beneath my feet was satisfying as I made my way over to the Orangery, keen to find a few more white flowers from their expansive gardens. I wanted to find a perfect single white rose. While I'd been researching plants and flowers for my illustrator job, I'd read quite a bit about white roses. They were often included in the bridal bouquet because they represented young love, new beginnings and eternal loyalty—not to mention purity, innocence, and youthfulness. A hard-working rose, that's for sure. A single white rose would complete the decorations with a nod toward the wedding vows Lauren and Ryan would be taking in a few hours.

Soon the Orangery came into view, its white frame glowing in the morning light, its huge panes of glass shimmering and refractive, the wisteria bright purple and plump against the blue sky.

I could only imagine how nervous Lauren must be feeling, rushing about her mom's house, doing all those last-minute beauty treatments: perfect makeup, hair styled and set. Just thinking about it made my heart beat a little quicker. All eyes would be on her today. The pressure would be immense. In a way, it was exactly how I felt while filming was happening. No matter how stressed I actually was, my face had to stay frown-free. I couldn't garble my words or *um* and *er*. Well, in case anyone ever did actually ask me to marry them, at least I'd be a pro at smiling through my nerves.

I headed in the direction of the gardens, the pretty little stream to my left. It looked even more lovely than I remembered.

The flowerbeds had been perfectly manicured, everything arranged to look timeless in that typical Broomewode fashion. It didn't take long for me to find the roses, their petals sumptuous, stems long and elegant. I'd brought my manicure scissors and set about choosing the most beautiful bloom.

"Morning over there," a voice rang out.

I looked up and recognized one of the girls from the Broomewode Hall kitchen. She was carrying my cake toward the Orangery. Jessica really had worked her magic, as the cake stood on top of a freshly polished silver stand that looked both old and stately. The silver glinted in the morning sun, and even the lavender sugar flowers gleamed on the cake.

"Isn't it the perfect day for a wedding?" I said in return. "Do you need some help carrying that?"

"No. Don't worry. I won't drop it. They always get me to carry the tricky things as I'm so sure-footed."

I couldn't watch. I wished she hadn't even put the idea of dropping the cake in my head. I wanted to run over and take it from her and carry the thing myself, but she was a catering professional, and of the two of us, I was bound to be the klutzier.

She kept chatting when I really wanted all her attention on carrying my beautiful cake. "You've done a lovely job. They'll be so pleased."

"Thanks," I said, because I had to say something when the woman had so kindly complimented my work. "Is everything under control in the kitchen?"

"Aye, yes. Unless we get the food perfect, that matron of honor will have *my* head on a plate."

I laughed and told her I'd join her inside to decorate the cake in a moment. My heart soared a little at that—*my* cake, *my* creation, was going to be the crowning moment of the wedding feast later today. I'd put money on Ryan and Lauren being the type of couple to feed cake to each other, really hamming up the moment for the crowd—and the camera. When Jessica had called me and asked me—I mean commanded me—to do this job, I'd been so worried about not having enough time and messing it up. But now I was glad I'd done it. I'd met some lovely people and helped make their happy day extra special. I doubted most cake bakers got invited to the wedding reception. Just another perk of being part of a TV reality show. In a way, *I* was the lucky one today.

I snipped the stems of two lovely white roses.

I'd get the cake finished, and then it was job done. I was on the home run. Bundt cakes and getting myself back into the top three for this weekend's episode of the baking contest was all I had to think about.

I stood up and started toward the Orangery.

A terrible scream rippled through air. It had to be the girl who'd been carrying my cake. My heart nearly bounded out of my chest. She must have dropped the cake. I broke into a run as my hopes for a perfect cake came crashing down.

The girl was still screaming and backing up as she did so. She sounded hysterical. I gulped. Maybe she hadn't dropped the cake. I'd let my thoughts wander thinking about love and marriage and cakes. What if I'd started to move Stupid Cupid around again? What if he'd fallen plump-cheek-first into the cake? I had visions of mushed buttercream, crumbled sponge. Me and my crazy unharnessed powers. Or could it be Gerry, despite his protest of innocence? If he'd ruined my beautiful creation in the name of a prank, well, I would kill him—if he wasn't already dead.

The girl's back was silhouetted against the light. She let out another wail as I raced over. I wanted to tell her to stop. We'd figure something out. I baked cakes under pressure all the time; I'd manage to salvage this disaster.

Suddenly, the overhead lights flicked on, and I turned to find Benedict coming in behind me. He'd thought to turn on the overhead lights.

The girl backed toward us, slowly. And that's when I saw the body fully laid out on the ground. It was Ryan. He was on his back, a great pool of blood spooling on the polished parquet floor behind his head. She'd dropped the wedding cake next to him. Now it was nothing but messy dollops of buttercream and sponge. A lavender sugar leaf had fallen loose and landed in the congealing blood. The silver stand had rolled against the body.

I went closer and bent to check Ryan's pulse. His skin was stone cold. He was dead. And by the looks of it, something— or someone—had bashed his head in from behind. I felt despair and anger and fear like a cloud over him. "I'm so sorry," I whispered. "This should have been the best day of your life."

Benedict had his phone out, and I could hear him speaking to the police, explaining where we were and what had happened. He sounded calm and in control, but the shock was evident in his expression: wide eyes, pale skin, perspiration gathering at his temples.

"Dead?" he asked me.

I nodded, and he passed the information on.

I looked again at Ryan's body. He was wearing the same white linen shirt as last night, the silver chain higher on his throat now. Benedict finished his call and told me that the police were on their way. They'd asked him to lock the Orangery for safety. I watched him walk over to the door and take out the keys. His hand was trembling, and he had trouble getting the lock to turn. Part of me wanted to rush over and relieve him of the task; the other half was rooted to the ground in shock. Whatever had happened here was no accident, and what should have been the most perfect day had turned into a nightmare.

There was a throbbing pain in my thumb, and I remembered the roses I'd picked to decorate the cake with. I'd held onto the stems so hard, the thorns had pricked me. I looked down at my palm. I'd crushed the head of the rose in my fist. Its white petals were scattered on the floor, speckled with my blood.

The poor kitchen girl was still crying. I went to put my arm around her, and she sobbed into my neck. Benedict came and stood next to us. We looked at each other. He said what I was thinking. "Who is going to tell the bride?"

CHAPTER 7

*T*he moments before Detective Inspector Hembly
and Sergeant Lane arrived seemed to go on
forever. Time slowed right down. All I could hear was the
girl's shuddering breaths (I managed to coax her name from
her mid-sob; it was Emily) and the thud-thud of my own
heartbeat.

I surveyed the image before me like it was a still from a
film. I turned the scene to black and white, to distance myself
perhaps, imagining Ryan as a golden Hollywood heartthrob,
his white shirt part of a three-piece suit, his blond hair
bleached out by the sepia tones. In this way, I tried to divert
my mind, turn it toward something less terrible. Something
more practical maybe, like who could have done such a
thing?

*Please don't let anyone from the wedding party show up before
the police.* I knew I wouldn't be able to find the right words to
explain what had happened—or any words, for that matter.
But Benedict's voice brought me back to reality.

"It's going to be okay, Poppy." His voice was firm, as

though he could promise such a thing, but it did give me comfort.

"Emily," he said, "go back to the kitchen and ask Katie to make you a cup of tea. Tell them..." He looked at me then, but I was as unsure as he was what we should say. "Tell them there's been an accident. No one's to come near the Orangery or speak to any of the wedding party."

"But Jessica...?" she managed to utter.

"Put Jessica or anyone else who calls straight through to my mobile. Do you understand?"

She nodded, her tears drying. I thought she'd be better now that she had something to do and could escape this terrible scene.

"Mind what I said. Not a word to anyone."

"Can I tell Katie?"

"Yes," he said, to my surprise. "Have her take you to her sitting room and you can tell her there. She's good in a crisis. She'll know how to handle the staff and caterers." He paused. "And Katie's to call me if she needs to."

Emily swiped her shaking hands over her face and then left. I thought of the cheerful greeting I'd had when I arrived, how much we'd both looked forward to this day of joy and how quickly the day had turned to tragedy.

Although it was grim, once Emily had left, I went back to Ryan's body. I knew better than to touch anything, but I wanted to take a closer look at his head wound.

There was a huge gash on the side of his forehead that must have stretched round even further. When I'd checked his pulse earlier, the skin was cool to the touch. He couldn't have died recently—it must have happened sometime last night.

A rap at the door prevented me from deducing anything more.

Benedict sprang back into action and went to unlock the door. I spotted Sergeant Lane immediately, dressed in navy trousers and white shirt. Detective Hembly looked as formal as ever in his starched shirt and pressed gray trousers. They stepped inside, and I watched Benedict shake both their hands with a hearty grip. Behind the officers were three other people I didn't recognize, but since Benedict would have called this in as a murder, I knew that there were very soon going to be teams of technicians and officers on the premises.

Poor Ryan. He'd expected to be the center of attention today, but not like this.

DI Hembly broke away from the group and approached the body. He took a long look at Ryan and then stepped toward me, nodding in recognition. "Poppy. You found the body?"

"No. One of the kitchen staff did. I was here to decorate the wedding cake."

We both glanced at the smashed cake, which was sending scents of lemon and coconut into the air.

Benedict told him he'd sent Emily back to the hall to stop anyone else from coming to the Orangery. "I've asked her to tell no one but Katie Donegal, our cook, what's happened. Katie's a sensible woman. She'll keep the kitchen in order."

I was pleased that he spoke so well of Katie Donegal. I only wished I could get the trusted old servant to open up to me about Valerie.

Sgt. Lane had been talking with the woman from forensics and the photographer. Now they went over to the body and began to take pictures. The forensics technician set down a black doctor's bag and pulled out some equipment. She began collecting evidence from the scene, swabbing fibers and hairs and taking a sample of the blood around Ryan's head—all the while jotting things down in a spiral notebook. No doubt she'd perform tests on these samples later in a lab. It must be such a strange job, to see dead bodies every day, and even stranger to be the one photographing them. I mean, how do you train to do that? Do you go to art school? Police academy?

"Poppy?" Sgt. Lane looked at me expectantly, a small smile on his face. Oh, those dimples. He must have been asking me something while I zoned out about crime scenes. *Keep it together, Pops.*

"Can you talk us through what you saw today?" he asked kindly.

For a moment I was dumbstruck, as if the reality of what had happened wouldn't be true if I didn't put it into words. But then my instincts kicked in, and I felt myself handling the story of what happened almost expertly, describing my morning picking flowers, seeing Emily carrying the cake to the Orangery, the scream, the body. Once I got going, the words flew out of me. And then I realized none of this explained why I came to be here today. So I backtracked— about how Jessica had contacted me and asked me to bake the wedding cake—I threw in the detail about Lauren's sick aunt—and that I'd met the whole wedding party yesterday, bridesmaids and groomsmen, and that I couldn't believe that this perfect day had been shattered by something so brutal.

As I spoke, the morning sun grew brighter, and now the Orangery was bathed in warm, white light. The beauty of the place seemed cruel.

I took a breath.

Sgt. Lane was still scribbling away in his notebook, taking down every detail.

"Thank you, Poppy," he said softly. "That's very helpful. It's good to get a full picture of the events leading up to the death, too. Anything you might know about the bridal party can help us understand more about what happened here."

Sgt. Lane turned now to Benedict. I hadn't noticed he'd been standing by my side this whole time.

"I heard the screaming, too," he said. "I was coming up to check that everything was all set."

"You supervise the catering yourself, Lord Winford?" he asked. I couldn't tell if he was being curious or sarcastic. Maybe a bit of both.

"This is a working estate, Sergeant Lane. Between death duties and the expenses of keeping Broomewode Hall operating, we all have to pitch in. So, yes, I came to check the Orangery. The kitchen staff didn't need my help with the canapés." Ooh, he could be politely sarcastic too.

"And you heard screams."

"So I came running," he continued. "I thought she'd dropped the cake or found a mouse in the venue or something. Not...this." He gestured at the body. "I called you both straightaway."

"You did well," DI Hembly said, joining us. "The scene appears to be undisturbed. But as yet, there's no sign of a murder weapon."

And then I remembered my first thoughts when I'd heard the screaming. Had I moved the cupid statue with my powers? I glanced over at the pedestal where the statue belonged. It was empty. I spun round, scanning the room for the cupid.

"What is it?" Sgt. Lane asked, watching me gyrate like an inept ballerina.

"The cupid. It's missing."

"I beg your pardon?" DI Hembly asked. "Cupid?"

They were all looking at me blankly. "Cupid. The bridesmaids made me rub his belly yesterday for good luck. In love, I mean. It's a ritual, apparently."

Sgt. Lane and DI Hembly raised their eyebrows in perfect unison.

"She means the cupid statue," Benedict said, saving me from sounding like a total loon. He pointed at the pedestal. "There should be a marble statue of a cupid right there. It's been in my family for generations. We decided to put it in the Orangery as a little bonus for the weddings booked here, but it has a lot of sentimental value. My mother will be furious."

Oh great. I'd managed to get my powers tangled up with a Champney family heirloom. Well done, Poppy.

But was the missing cupid actually my fault? Could I have moved it in my sleep at night so it accidentally bashed the groom's head in? I racked my brains, trying to dredge up any memories of dreams (or nightmares) that I might have had. Had I become angry with Stupid Cupid and used my powers to move it about—even from the safety of my bed? I shuddered. I was in way over my witchy head if my powers had become that unruly.

I swallowed and turned to Benedict, dreading what I was about to ask. "Could the statue be heavy enough to...bludgeon a man to death?"

"Absolutely," he said, looking grim.

"We should call for backup," Sgt. Lane said. "Put a couple of men on the grounds to search for the statue. If it was the murder weapon, it might have been dumped nearby."

It took all my strength not to put my head in my hands. *Please don't let this be all my fault.*

DI Hembly went to make the phone call, and Sgt. Lane said we should make our way back to the inn.

"Who's going to tell Lauren?" I asked. "She's at her mom's house, probably getting dressed as we speak."

"We'll go over there now. Hembly will," Sgt. Lane said. "DI Hembly is very good in these situations. Calm and reassuring." He paused and turned back. "Did the bride and groom seem happy about the upcoming wedding?"

Benedict and I exchanged a glance, and both of us nodded. "Ryan bent my ear last night about how lucky he was," Benedict said. "He'd had a few too many drinks and got a bit maudlin, to be honest, but he seemed genuinely in love."

"And when I saw Lauren earlier in the day, she was the same. She glowed with happiness. Her biggest fear was that for some reason her groom might not show up." I shrugged. "Bridal nerves."

I left the Orangery with a heavy heart, pausing at the door to take in the scene one last time. So much love and care had gone into its decoration: the strings of fairy lights and purple ribbon; tables set up for the grand feast, flowers at their center. I sighed at the orange trees, plump now with fruit after Jessica's instruction for more. There would be no celebrating today. It would be a day of sorrow and mourning.

Benedict said goodbye and returned to Broomewode Hall to inform his parents about what had happened. I could imagine Lady Frome's distaste at a murder happening on her grounds. *And what about the parquet flooring?* I could hear her ask. *I do so hope the blood stains come out.*

Sgt. Lane held open the door for me as I left. The sun hit my face, warming my skin. "Most of the wedding party is at the inn," I said to Sgt. Lane as we stepped out. I told him about meeting the group last night, the rambunctious laughter and drinking. How much joy there'd been in the group. But then I remembered that wasn't strictly true. The tension between Ryan and Lauren's brother, George, was palpable. And what about that conversation between him and Julius, one of the groomsmen? Something about money? I was about to say as much to Sgt. Lane when I stopped. Reporting little tiffs like this was tantamount to suggesting motive. I had to take care and be certain of the facts before I implicated near-strangers in a murder investigation. I'd do a little detective work of my own when we got back to the inn. Just a few questions, nothing that would disturb my focus for the baking contest...which, of course, was due to start filming tomorrow.

CHAPTER 8

*B*ack at the inn, Sgt. Lane and I parted ways so that he could gather the wedding party together. I couldn't imagine being the messenger of such awful news. My thoughts went immediately to Harry, Ryan's father. He would be shattered.

"I might need to ask you a few more questions later, Poppy," he said softly, "so if you can stick around the inn, that would be great."

I assured him that I had no intention of going anywhere.

Watching Sgt. Lane disappear into the pub, I lingered in the hallway, uncertain whether to retreat to my room or try to find Eve and talk things through. I wanted to know if she'd also noticed any tensions in the wedding party—and whether those tensions might be enough motive for a terrible murder. If only Elspeth was here. She'd know exactly what to say and do. I touched the amethyst necklace and tried to focus on conjuring her lovely face, those kind eyes, her knowing look. I tried to summon that jolt of electricity, willing it to rise up in my body and bring forth Elspeth. I squeezed my eyes tighter still, keeping my hand on the necklace.

"Er, Poppy? Are you feeling okay?"

Not electricity but panic flooded through me. That was *not* Elspeth's voice. I opened my eyes slowly, as if that might change anything.

Florence stared back at me, her eyes agog. "What on earth are you doing?" she said, laughing that rich throaty laugh of hers. "You look like you're trying to raise the dead."

"Funny you should say that," I murmured, not yet daring to speak the truth.

She kissed both my cheeks in swift succession in that elegant Italian manner of hers and then stood back, looking at me strangely. "Funny I should say what?"

I told her she might need to sit down before I told her about my week.

"It's never straightforward with you, is it, Poppy Wilkinson? I've been chained to the kitchen all week, head to toe in flour. Didn't even manage to wash and blow-dry my hair until last night. European Bakes should be my week, right? The pressure is too much." She widened her eyes in dramatic fashion as she stopped for breath. "But from the looks of you, you've been through the cake-mixer yourself." She gestured at her luggage—two suitcases and a dry cleaner's zip-bag. "Give me a hand, will you, darling? I'll make us some tea in my room, and you can tell me all about it."

There was something about Florence's blustery tour-de-force personality that I found weirdly soothing in times of crisis. Maybe she could help me make sense of what had happened today. I picked up both suitcases and followed her up the stairs. It was the first time I'd ever seen her wearing jeans, although they were nothing like my old stonewashed Levis; hers were pristine white, high on the waist and wide-legged, a black camisole tucked into the top of a black woven belt. Her chestnut curls tumbled down her back as she sashayed through the corridor.

"Hold on—you can make tea in your room?"

"Of course, darling," she replied, turning to face me before she opened the door. "I asked for a kettle, two mugs, and a proper selection of teas. Don't tell me you haven't demanded the same?"

I had to laugh. I obviously hadn't demanded anything. Though, to be fair, the kitchen was always willing to supplement Gateau's diet with treats.

"I also make liberal use of the laundry service."

"There's a laundry service?" I asked. Where had I been?

She looked at me like she was wondering where I'd been too. "I can't bear wearing the same clothes two days in a row for filming. I use the overnight laundry service." She went to her closet, and there was a hanger with a plastic bag with "laundry" printed on it. I'd always assumed that was so guests could put their dirty laundry in to take home, but Florence laughed at me. "No, silly. You put whatever you need laundered in the bag. Fill out this card to say how you want it laundered and when you need it. I always have my clothes back the next day before breakfast. Sometimes, I throw on a bit of flour over my fresh clothes the next day so it's not too obvious."

I laughed. But I was seriously thinking I might use the service too, especially if I'd had a really messy Saturday.

Florence's room was a bit larger than mine. Two damask armchairs sat on either side of the sash window, a round coffee table between them, with tea-making things in a small wicker box.

I sank into the armchair and listened as Florence chatted idly about her week. Her room was on the opposite side of the inn to me, and the window looked out onto the White-beam trees, which flanked either side of the path to the inn, their puffy leaves swaying gently in the breeze. Beyond them was the path that led to the woodland, and I remembered walking with Elspeth that chilly evening to my first magic circle. It seemed like eons ago.

Florence's agent had talked to her about a commercial, and they were very hopeful that once this season of the baking contest was wrapped, Florence could transfer her newfound popularity to her own cooking show. "Because I am fluent in both Italian and English, Poppy, they want to pitch it to both countries. Isn't that exciting? And don't think I'll forget you. I shall have you as a guest baker. Though not, of course, in Italian."

I was suitably impressed, or tried to be, though my thoughts were, obviously, obsessing on Ryan's murder. I felt a terrible heaviness on my chest, as though the marble cupid had taken up residence there.

Florence set the tea down. "Now, your turn to spill. What's happened?"

I opened my mouth to tell her everything, knowing that if I told her she couldn't tell anyone, I could rely on her, when there was a knock at the door. Florence rolled her eyes and called out that it was open.

It was Hamish. I stood and hugged him. His hair had

been buzzed closer to his head, army-style, and he would have looked even more tough and no-nonsense than usual if it wasn't for that broad grin of his. His gray hoodie softened the look, too, and he looked comfortable in jeans. I had a hard time imagining Hamish in his police officer uniform, though that must be what he wore all week. In fact, it was kind of hard to imagine *anyone* on the show in their regular life. When we were in Broomewode Village, it was like the real world didn't exist.

"Sit down, Hamish," Florence said, patting a green pouf. "How are you? Poppy was about to tell me something big."

They both looked at me expectantly.

Florence always had to make things even more dramatic than they were already. I braced myself and then said, "There's been a murder."

Florence drew in a sharp breath. Hamish stared at me. "What? Not another one." When a cop sounded shocked about murder...

He was right. This was one murder too many. I was beginning to think I didn't only draw ghosts to me but unnatural deaths as well.

"Tell us everything," Florence said. Her eyes glittered. She reminded me of old cartoons, when characters had dollar signs pop up in their eyes like slot machines—hers were like that, but with *drama, drama, drama.*

I recounted what I'd already told Sgt. Lane, and as I retold the events of the past few days, I combed through the details again, trying to find some clue as to why Ryan might have been murdered. I described the wedding party: the chilled-out, beautiful bride-to-be, Lauren; her high-maintenance matron of honor, Jessica; the twin bridesmaids hoping to find their true love; the handsome groom, Ryan, and his life-of-the-party father, Harry. Then I told them about the cupid statue—leaving out the details of my love ritual, of course; that would have been way too embarrassing—and how it was missing. It was heavy enough to cause a serious head injury.

They both listened intently, Hamish with his serious police officer face, Florence seeming to enjoy it more as a story than real life. I figured Hamish was the perfect person to help me explore the possibility of the tensions I'd witnessed over drinks last night.

"But there's something troubling me," I confessed to them both. "I was with the wedding party last night while they were doing tequila shots and—"

"*You* were doing tequila shots?" Florence interrupted, incredulous. "Without us?"

"I only had a gin and tonic." I laughed. "But that's not what's important here. Despite the shots, the wedding party weren't exactly carefree and celebrating. I overheard snippets of conversations between the groom and his friend about money. I couldn't catch all of it, but it sounded tense—like Ryan had lent him cash and was asking for it back. The other guy looked sick to his stomach."

"Never loan money to friends," Hamish said. "If only you knew the scuffles I've seen between family and friends over cash. It's never worth it."

"Neither a borrower nor a lender be," Florence said as though she were on stage projecting to the back row. "I was in *Hamlet* once. I played Ophelia. It was a dreary part. Poor dear goes mad."

I waited politely until she'd finished her Shakespearean recollections. "But that wasn't the only strange thing that happened. The bride's brother, George, showed up and got right in Ryan's face. He implied that Ryan had been unfaithful and he warned him never to stray again now that he and Lauren were getting married."

At that, Florence's dark eyebrows shot up. "Scoundrel," she said. "Lauren sounds like a catch, and here's her husband who isn't even her husband yet, betraying her." She turned to Hamish. "Why do men do this? Why can't they keep it in their pants?"

Hamish held his hands up. "Don't ask me. I'm the model boyfriend, when I get the chance, that is."

"Oh, you're a catch, Hamish. The right woman will come along any day now and snatch you right up."

Hello? I'm in the middle of talking about a murder investigation here.

"Guys, guys, that's so not the point right now."

"Poppy's right. Less talk about my love life and more focus on the matter at hand," Hamish said.

"The muddy death," Florence said ominously in her best Shakespearean voice.

I looked again at the view from Florence's window, so serene and beautiful. A perfect day for a wedding. I shuddered. "What can we do?" I asked Hamish.

He shook his head. "Obviously it's not good that two people in the wedding party seemed to have bad blood with Ryan. But that doesn't mean we can accuse them of murder. We need more to go on."

Hamish was right. He was so clearheaded.

Florence suggested we head downstairs to the pub for a

coffee. "Nothing like a shot of espresso to kick-start the brain."

Hamish led the way, and Florence locked the door behind us, checking it twice. "If there's a murderer on the loose, I'm not taking any chances," she whispered.

My mind flashed back to the warning note, which I still hadn't gotten to the bottom of. The thought that someone wanted me off the show that much sent shivers down my spine. But I could only deal with one thing at a time—right now, murder trumped a warning note.

I was hoping to see Eve in the pub, but a young man I hadn't met before was behind the bar. Florence's eyes lit up. "I'll get us those coffees," she said quickly.

Hamish raised an eyebrow at me, and I smiled. But that smile quickly disappeared as I realized some of the wedding party had gathered here too, and from their faces, I knew that Sgt. Lane had delivered the bad news. I gestured for Hamish to sit with me at a corner table, out of sight, and talked him through the group.

There was Harry, the groom's father. His sparkling blue eyes were wet with tears, and he was staring into the depths of an untouched pint. A man I hadn't seen before was next to him, twisting his hands, his eyes trained on the window. Both men were pale and wore matching harrowed expressions. My heart went out to them. I couldn't imagine the depths of their sadness. Today should have been the beginning of a new chapter, not the closing of a book.

But then Jessica arrived, and behind her was Lauren, and it was like my heart dropped through my body to my feet. Both women had been made up and had their hair done for the wedding. They looked beautiful. It was too much. This should have been the happiest day of Lauren's life. She ran over to Harry and threw her arms around him. I could hear him make soothing noises as she sobbed. She pulled away and looked at him, tears streaming down her pretty face. "I don't know what to do with myself. I couldn't stay at home."

Her blond hair had been curled, and it hung around her face. Harry brushed it away from her cheek. "I've got no words," he said quietly. "My precious baby boy. How could this happen?" At that, Lauren burst into tears again, and Harry said he'd fetch her a brandy. Jessica was holding hands with the man I hadn't recognized but now I realized must be her husband, Joe. Lauren sat next to him, and he held her hand, too. The three of them sat that way as if frozen.

I felt the ache in my throat, and I wanted to cry too. As terrible as this day was, at least they had each other.

Hamish and I watched the scene in silence until Florence returned with our coffee. She set down a steaming cup in front of me, and I cradled the porcelain, letting the hot liquid warm my hands. Lauren's and Harry's grief had chilled me to the bone. I was more determined than ever that whoever had committed this ghastly crime should be brought to justice.

I took a sip of my coffee. "There's Sergeant Lane," Hamish said, pointing in the direction of the bar. "I'm going to have a word with him, see what information I can get."

I nodded. As a fellow police officer, Sgt. Lane would likely trust Hamish with information about the investigation.

"His name is Darius, in case you were wondering," Florence said coyly.

"Pardon?" I was watching the wedding party, soon to be a funeral party.

"The sexy barman. He's just started. Here for the summer season. He's from Greece."

I didn't know how Florence could think about romance right now.

"Oh, don't look at me like that," she said. "You've got to strike while the iron's hot, as they say."

I didn't want to think about iron striking anything. I'd seen enough head wounds for one day.

Hamish returned, looking grim. "Time of death was between midnight and three a.m."

I was right; Hamish *was* trusted with sensitive information.

"How do you know?" Florence asked indignantly.

"Professional courtesy between police officers," Hamish said.

"Anything else?" I asked.

"He was drunk."

"I could have told you that," I said. Goodness knows how many more tequila shots Harry insisted on buying after I'd excused myself from the group. "Have they found the murder weapon?"

"No. But death was definitely caused by blunt force trauma to the head."

I winced, thinking of Cupid as a killer.

Florence said, "So someone bashed the groom over the head the night before the wedding." She shook her head so her long hair danced. "I've been known to throw things in a lover's tiff, but someone really wanted that man dead. Do you think the timing's significant? I mean, why kill him before he gets married?"

Hamish nodded at her approvingly, and it was an excellent question. "Things change when a man marries. It's a legal contract."

Florence nodded and quoted, "And with all my worldly goods I thee endow."

"Exactly," Hamish said. "Perhaps someone else had dibs on Ryan's worldly goods." He looked at me. "Was he wealthy, do you know?"

I shook my head. "No idea."

Florence pulled out her phone. "We shall do a search. What's the surname?" I stared at her, and she laughed. "I do it all the time if I'm interested in a man. I like to know what his job is, what clubs he belongs to. You can find out a great deal about someone in an astonishingly short amount of time."

"Ryan Blandford," I told her, and she went to work.

Hamish drained his coffee cup. He took the little cookie that came on the saucer and tapped it on the tabletop. "But what I don't understand is why the killer didn't put the victim's body out in the grounds amongst the rocks? It would look like he fell while inebriated and bashed in his own head. Somebody could have got away with murder."

I shivered. Trust a cop to figure out how to get away with murder.

Florence leaned in. "Perhaps the killer wasn't strong enough. What if it was a crime of passion?" she asked with a flourish, sweeping her elegant hands in the air. Her nails were painted blood-red. I shivered.

"Could be, I suppose," he said. "But who would commit a crime of passion against him?" He glanced over at the bride, still weeping against Harry's shoulder. "The bride doesn't look good for it."

Florence squinted at the wedding party. "Don't be fooled

by appearances. I could do a better job of acting grief-stricken than she is."

Lauren was sobbing and pale. What did Florence have in mind, I wondered. Loud wailing and rending her clothes?

"Ah, here we are," Florence said. "His business profile says he's a banker in London. Went to the London School of Economics." She was nodding as though he was passing her test so far. "Belongs to a sports club and a business club."

She did some more searching. "Ah, his Instagram account shows him and a pretty girl. Holidays are nice but not over the top." She glanced up. "He earns good money, but his best years are ahead of him. Rents a house in London, doesn't own. Solid middle-class chap, I'd say. No hint of a family fortune. Father's in insurance. I'd say there's no wealth there."

"That was amazing," I said, really impressed.

She gave me a small, smug smile. "I don't like to waste my time."

"Didn't you say the brother didn't approve of the match?" Hamish asked.

"That's right," I said. "It was pretty uncomfortable, actually. He still showed for drinks with everyone, but he was surly. And he wasn't trying to be quiet warning Ryan not to mess up again. He made it sound like Ryan had been unfaithful, but he was also pretty drunk."

Florence said, "Maybe that gave him the perfect alibi, to show up to the drinks, to be vocal about his disapproval. After all that, no one would think he was mad enough to commit murder." Maybe she had a good point there.

Hamish seemed to think so, too. He changed tack. "Let's not forget about this other guy—did you say his name was Julius?"

I nodded. Something had definitely happened between those two, and it sounded like the issue was money––a sticky subject between friends. Julius might have been in Ryan's debt, but was it bad enough to get rid of his old friend entirely? Surely they could have worked something out. A payment plan of sorts.

I was about to float this with Hamish when suddenly a wave of calm flooded through me. I looked up, and there was Elspeth and Jonathon standing by our table. But instead of the friendly faces I was used to seeing, they were frowning.

"We heard the terrible news," Elspeth said. "Another murder in Broomewode. I can't believe it." I was so happy to see them. I had so many questions, especially for Elspeth, but I'd have to wait until we were away from prying eyes to ask if she knew anything about telekinesis.

"But don't get so carried away by this tragedy that you all lose sight of the baking contest," she warned. She was looking straight at me. "You've got to have your head in the competition."

Jonathon nodded.

Elspeth looked at me quite sternly. "That goes doubly for you, Poppy. I want your mind on European Bakes. Not murder."

I swallowed hard. Being publicly told off by the great Elspeth Peach did not feel good. I solemnly promised that I'd do my best this week, and Hamish and Florence chimed in that they would, too. A moment ago, the three of us had to been trying to solve a murder, but now we sat ashamed of ourselves like naughty schoolkids.

"Right then," Elspeth said. "We'll look forward to some

excellent baking this weekend." And with that shot, she and Jonathon moved on.

"Crikey," Hamish said as soon as they were out of earshot. "Elspeth Peach always makes me feel like I'm back in school. And I'm failing."

I knew exactly what he meant.

CHAPTER 9

"*P*oppy, stop grimacing. What if the wind changes and your face stays that way?"

Gina tugged again at my ponytail, and I laughed. She was the only person who could tame my thick brown locks into a sleek ponytail—but my goodness, it hurt when she whipped my flyaways into shape. I obeyed her orders and kept still until she was finished, taking the opportunity to close my eyes to the tent's bright lights.

So much had happened over the past few days that it felt like an age since I'd last been on set. Even with my eyes closed, every corner of the set was embedded in my very being. The vast expanse of crisp white calico above my head, the gorgeous green lawns of the estate beyond it. Beneath my feet were the long planks of polished pine, where I hoped I wouldn't goof up and drop my cake. My nerves couldn't take another creation splattered across the ground.

"All done," Gina said. "Now just a final slick of gloss, and you'll be ready to knock them dead."

Gina spun me round and painted my lips with something

that smelled like cinnamon. I thought my beautifying was over, but then she began fiddling with my earrings. "Let me set these straight," she murmured. The earrings were my favorite: two gold ginkgo leaves set with green stones on a gold chain so that they dangled near my shoulders. I'd held back from wearing them on the show, worried I'd get them caught in my hair as I furiously stirred some cake mix, but Gina's sleek ponytail should keep me out of harm's way. Besides, they matched my green shirtdress perfectly.

I watched Gina's face as she concentrated, trying to focus on her familiar, calm features. The kindness in her eyes. Anything but the nerves coursing through my body. By now, I was used to the pressure. I wasn't the newbie on a TV set anymore. I knew the ropes. I knew that Gina had to heavily powder my face to make sure I didn't shine on camera; I knew the best place for my mic pack to be clipped to stop it from showing on screen. Okay, so that might not have made me a seasoned professional like Elspeth or Jonathon, but I was learning the ropes. So why did I feel so on edge?

"Chin up, Pops," Gina said, putting a hand on my shoulder. Then she leaned in so no one could overhear her. "You've got this. I've tasted your Bundt cake. It's a winner."

"Shh. Don't jinx it."

She gave me a knowing look. "Now go out there and show them what you've got."

I stood, pulled my shoulders back and took a deep breath. There was nothing for it now but to bake my little socks off.

Daniel was waiting for Gina to give his nose a powder. I asked him what he was going to bake today. He told me he'd gone on holiday to Austria with his family last year and the children fell in love with Austrian peach cookies. "They're like hollowed-out biscuits, filled with a sweet peach pulp and then decorated to look like a miniature peach."

"Sounds delicious," I told him. They sounded great but a challenge to pull off in our strict time limitation.

I made my way through the tent, waving at Hamish and Maggie as I passed. Having my workstation placed in the middle had its benefits. I felt cushioned by my friends, and listening to their busy preparations calmed me down. Florence was nowhere to be seen, of course. No doubt she was still at the inn, putting the final touches to another fabulous outfit.

I touched my pristine counter and began to unpack my supplies, arranging them in size order, and laying out my recipes.

"Hello, darling." Florence swept into the tent, her auburn curls bouncing prettily. She flashed her perfect white teeth. "Always late, I know. But all this"—she gestured at her denim jumpsuit, belted tightly at the waist, the frill of white shirt peeking out at the neck and sleeves—"takes a while." She kissed both my cheeks. "Those earrings are to die for."

I grimaced, grateful for the compliment, but her choice of words was a little too on the nose.

"Sorry," she said. "No more talk of death or dying. Let's keep our eye on the prize."

She began unpacking her ingredients.

"Well, you'll be safe," I said. "European Bakes week was made for you. What Italian treat will you be cooking up today?"

But Florence shook her head. "Too obvious." Instead, she'd chosen to do something Turkish. *Sekerpare,* she said. "It means 'a piece of sweetness.' Good talking point, right?"

I told her that I'd never heard of those before.

"They're sweet and sticky cookies, made from semolina, flour and powdered sugar. They're baked until they turn an amazing golden brown color. Then you steep them in a lemony syrup. By the time they're ready to serve, they're so tender you can slice through them like butter." She paused and frowned. "But to get them to that point, I'll have to work double quick."

"If anyone can rise to a challenge, it's you," I said.

She was about to reply when Donald Friesen, the series producer, came on set with Fiona, the director. Donald's black hair was slicked back, and he wore a snappy gray suit and shiny black loafers. Even though we were old pros by now, he reminded us to continue being ourselves and act naturally. Act natural? Didn't he know that was the worst thing you could say to a room full of nervous people?

"Keep having fun, guys, and good luck," he added.

Donald let Fiona take center stage, and she cued in the presenters.

Arty and Jilly stepped forward. "Good morning, bakers," Arty said. "Or should I say, *bonjour. Buon giorno.*"

He turned to Jilly, who continued, *"Guten tag,* bakers. It's European Bakes this week, and the judges are looking for a certain *je ne sais quois."*

"Say what?" Arty replied.

Jilly turned and gave us a big grin. Her mass of red curls was piled on top of her head and, behind her square blue glasses, her eyes were lined in dark kohl.

"Now hopefully you all got good grades in geography at school, because this is a challenge which allows you to have more freedom than others you've been set. But this doesn't mean the pressure is off. If anything, it's time to impress. European-style."

Arty took over again. "Your first task is to produce a baked good that's famous in any European region of your choice. Over several martinis last night, Jonathon and Elspeth told me that they're looking for the wow factor today. Unusual flavor combinations and interesting historical stories are going to win them over."

There was a loud "AHEM." Elspeth emerged from the side of the tent and came to join Arty and Jilly. She was wearing a cream pencil skirt and crisp white shirt; a gold chunky necklace gave her smart outfit a more casual look. Her white hair had been swept into its signature chignon and her lips painted a deep pink. She looked wonderful.

"I think you'll find I was drinking an elderflower pressé—not a martini." She laughed.

Jonathon appeared then. "That was me getting into the martinis. You'll really need to impress today."

Jilly turned to us. "Bakers, we won't keep you from your mixing bowls a moment longer. On your marks, get set, bake."

I began weighing out my ingredients, keeping my eye glued to the electric scales. Even a few ounces over or under could make all the difference. I was determined not to make any silly mistakes. But I couldn't resist stealing a look at what the others were doing. Had anyone else chosen the Bundt cake? I couldn't see any Bundt tins, but that didn't mean I was out of the woods. I focused on creaming my butter and sugar.

Elspeth went to Florence first, and I listened to her talk about the sekerpare cookies. Florence was so good in front of the cameras. She never ummed or erred like the rest of us.

She made it look easy. "So the sekerpare is made in nearly every Turkish household, sold in every bakery and sweet shop, and you'll find it on most Turkish restaurant menus," Florence said, weighing out her ingredients. How she managed to multitask under pressure, I'd never know. "It's one of the most popular Turkish sweets after baklava. I'd really recommend eating it alongside your next espresso. Of course, it goes perfectly with a cup of Turkish coffee, too." She laughed that throaty laugh of hers. She began to knead her dough by hand. "You have to do this bit slowly, otherwise the dough will crack and separate in the oven."

"And we don't want that," Elspeth said, smiling.

"Naturally. Each piece should keep its shape. But the real test will be when I add the syrup. The cookies need to soak it all up without crumbling."

"I'd wish you luck," Elspeth said, "but I don't think you need it."

Oh man, I wish Elspeth would bestow me with such words of encouragement. But as my luck would have it, Jonathon was heading toward me. Despite getting to know him better over the last few weeks, Jonathon was still intimidating, and I couldn't forget his reputation for being the tougher cookie to please. I started to grate my lemon zest into the now fluffy butter and sugar mix. Each step of this recipe was as routine to me as brushing my teeth. It was almost as if my hands were moving of their own accord. But I had to stay focused.

Jonathon appeared by my side. "I understand you're making a Bundt cake, Poppy, but with an unusual flavor combination. Can you talk me through it?"

The word unusual echoed in my ears. Wasn't lavender

and lemon a classic? I swallowed. "Well, to me, this is spring-time in a cake. The fresh lemon zest and lavender buds make for a light, herbaceous and refreshing cake. The flavors are subtle, not at all overpowering, and with any luck, my sponge will be moist. The crumb on this should be tender."

Jonathon nodded. His blue eyes still had that cheeky twinkle to them, but the rest of his face was serious. It was impossible to read whether he thought this sounded deli-cious or disastrous. "Tender crumb and a good balance of flavors. Absolutely what we're looking for. Good luck."

After wishing me luck, he moved over to Amara. I breathed out. That was short and sweet. Keep it together, Pops.

At least I wasn't the only one feeling nervous. I could hear Amara stumble over her words. Fiona, the director, called "cut," and they began filming her segment again. At breakfast, Amara had told me that she had a Swiss patient who made her a beautiful cherry cake every year. A *zuger kirschtorte*, she called it. She asked him for the recipe and then adapted it to her own taste. I'd never tasted one myself, but I'd seen them in fancy patisserie windows. It had a meringue base, ground and lightly roasted almonds and hazelnuts, and a cream filling flavored with cherry liqueur. And it had a great history. Amara told me that it was rumored to be Charlie Chaplin's and Audrey Hepburn's favorite dessert. What a great talking point for the cameras. Even if we did have to hear it twice. At least she sounded much smoother the second time.

Gaurav had also been with us at breakfast. A biking holiday he'd taken in Croatia last year had inspired his bake. He was making *buhtle,* which were Croatian jam-filled sweet rolls. Traditionally, they were filled with plum jam, but

Gaurav was using homemade apricot to balance out the sweetness of vanilla sugar with a more tart fruit. He said they were simple but time-intensive, so, like all of us, his challenge this morning was to work quickly without making any silly mistakes.

I began weighing out my dried lavender buds. Their scent was fresh and uplifting. I inhaled deeply. Susan Bentley had told me that lavender was a natural de-stresser. If I wasn't being filmed for a huge TV show, I'd probably stick my head right in the bowl. But instead I pretended that I was back in my own cottage kitchen, Mildred the ghost at my side (though in my fantasy, she was silent—I didn't need her criticism right now), using my own tools and listening to the radio.

It was in this delightful bubble that I passed the next hour, finishing my batter and sending my cake into the hands of the oven gods with a small well-wishing prayer. The only time I broke my concentration was to listen to Priscilla describe her bake. She was making a French *clafoutis*, one of my favorite ever desserts, so naturally my ears pricked up. It was an egg-based custard dish similar to a Dutch Baby, but silkier and more like a set custard in texture. It was pretty simple to make, so I hoped that she was doing something special with the ingredients to liven it up a bit.

The rest of the time went by in a blur, and when the timer clanged, I almost jumped out of my skin. Arty ordered us to stop what we were doing.

I joined the rest of the contestants as we made our way, trembling, to the judging table. Everyone had produced amazing bakes. Not a single obvious disaster on the table. Daniel's peach cookies looked incredible. So did Maggie's

Portuguese *tarte de amendoa,* which Elspeth was now cutting into. Like so many of today's bakes, they had a good story. As Portuguese legend went, the almond trees came to be part of the landscape of the southern region when an Arab prince became concerned that his wife from a northern country missed the snow so much, she was depressed. The prince ordered the planting of almond trees, whose blossoms created the illusion of fields covered with snow. Now almond was a hugely popular ingredient in Portugal, and its creamy, nutty flavor was a great match for pastry. Maggie was onto something there, and by the sounds of Jonathon's "mmms," the tart tasted as good as it looked.

"This is exquisite, Maggie," Elspeth said. "Perhaps the best almond tart I've ever had."

Whoa. That was some serious praise from the great Elspeth Peach. But could Daniel's cookies with her namesake peach tip the balance in his favor? They both seemed quite taken with his offering, but Jonathon claimed the filling to be overly sweet. Poor Daniel. His face showed how crushed he felt.

But I couldn't linger on his pain for too long—my plate was up next.

I held my breath as Jonathon and Elspeth took turns examining the texture of my sponge. "This glaze has been beautifully drizzled," Elspeth said, turning the plate right and left. "Like an abstract painting. And a gorgeous yellow color. The specks of purple in the sponge are lovely, too. It's very pleasing to look at. But the proof will be in the taste."

I watched as Elspeth took a delicate bite. After a moment that lasted at least seven centuries, she grinned. "Oh, how delightful. The balance of lavender and lemon is quite perfect. Fragrant and moist."

"Well done, Poppy," Jonathon said. "I quite agree with Elspeth. It has an excellent crumb and very good balance between the flavors. Very good indeed."

Thank goodness. Praise be. After being mediocre at best last week, I could feel a smile of pure relief spreading across my face.

They moved on, and I continued to listen, but without my heart lodged in my mouth. I'd done enough to impress the judges.

Priscilla was next. And Jonathon was less than complimentary. "There's nothing wrong with this *clafoutis,*" he was saying, "but at this stage of the competition, we'd expect something a little more...advanced from our contestants."

"Jonathon's right," Elspeth said. "It's quite lovely but too simple. You need to push yourself, Priscilla. Don't play it safe."

Priscilla's head fell, and she blushed deeply. My heart went out to her.

When Jilly announced that it was time to name the winners of this round, my heart began to pound. Jonathon delivered the news.

Priscilla was last, which was tough, as she always tried so hard. Still, she nodded bravely. I kept waiting to hear my name and it didn't come and didn't come and then...

"In third place, with her delightful Bundt cake, is Poppy." I was thrilled, not only to be in the top three but because I hadn't made anything move by accident. Gerry hadn't appeared either, which I considered another win.

It took all my self-control not to shout, *Hurray! I'd done it.*

After last week's mediocre performance, I'd redeemed myself. I barely heard Elspeth say Maggie in second place and then Gaurav's name.

We all rushed over to Gaurav. It was his second time in first place, but he still looked to be in shock.

"Well done, you," I said warmly, giving him a hug. "You deserve it!" I was delighted that Gaurav had won. He was trying to look modest, which made me like him even more. Maggie was glowing too, and who could blame her? I congratulated her and received my own modest share of compliments.

"Well done, Poppy," Florence said. "You sneaked into that top three." I smiled, but was there a hint of surprise in her voice? Her face was pretty as a picture, a wide smile, lively eyes, but I couldn't help but feel she wished it had been her and not me. She'd come in fifth. Maybe I'd do well to remember this was a competition.

Everyone tidied their workstations and then crowded around the lunch table. I was ravenous and loaded my plate. I needed serious fueling if I was going to have enough energy to make it through my second bake of the day.

Maggie suggested that we take our plates outside and picnic on the lawn. It was a gorgeous day—a shame to be stuck inside under hot lights. "Let's get some sun on our faces and fresh air in our lungs," she added. What a good idea.

But outside was not the calm and restful environment we'd had in mind. The usual group of people who liked to watch the filming was missing. Several police officers, including DI Hembly and Sgt. Lane, were roaming the lawns in the distance. Searching for the murder weapon?

"I see we're not the only ones having a technical challenge," Hamish said, watching them. No doubt he'd done his fair share of searching for clues.

By now, news of the tragic wedding day had spread. Although our cast and crew were shocked and saddened to hear about Ryan's murder, they'd been too focused on the competition for the news to really sink in. Besides, no one but me had even met Ryan. Seeing the police officers searching for clues on the grounds was a rude awakening. The high spirits of the group dampened, but we spread out around the tent anyway.

I bit into my wrap, but the taste soured in my mouth. I couldn't get the image of Ryan's lifeless body out of my mind. Hamish sensed my unease and sidled over to me. He lowered his voice to a whisper and told me that he'd spoken some more with Sgt. Lane this morning. "The groom's bank records show a transfer of money to one of the groomsmen."

"Let me guess. Julius," I said.

He nodded. "Not an insignificant amount."

I recalled the snippets of conversation I'd overheard at the pub. Julius had looked sick. Had Ryan asked Julius to pay back money he'd loaned him? And had Julius not been able to come up with the funds? Surely that wasn't reason enough to murder one of your oldest friends? Julius had given off a nervous energy, for sure. But murderous intentions on the eve of his old friend's wedding? It seemed a stretch.

"The police are really digging into him."

"Are you discussing the case?" Florence asked, wiggling over. Hamish repeated what he'd heard.

"Well, this morning, while I was running terribly late and scoffing down some toast, I heard several of the wedding party discussing how the groom had been super drunk. But his father—Harry, isn't it?—cut in and said that Ryan went up to bed at eleven p.m. A very reasonable hour. He hadn't told anyone he was walking up to the wedding venue." She shrugged and took a bite of her egg roll.

My mind flooded with questions. Why did he go up to the Orangery? Was he meeting someone? Was it just bad luck that he took a stroll late at night? Did he see something he shouldn't have? I had an overwhelming urge to visit the Orangery. No, more than that. It was like something was pulling at me, telling me to go.

I couldn't go now, not with a technical challenge still to get through. I'd made a good start this morning at improving my position in the competition. I couldn't drop the Bundt pan now. I made a pact with myself—smash it out of the park in the technical challenge, and then I could follow my instincts. Something was awry at the Orangery, and I was determined to get to the bottom of it.

CHAPTER 10

*B*ack in the tent, it was time for the technical challenge. The contestants were lined behind our workstations, poised and ready, nervous smiles pasted across our faces. Did anyone actually enjoy the pressure of the technical challenge? I found it more demanding to make exactly the same recipe as everyone else and then be forced to look at the judging table and see which one looked prettier or had the better crumb. I'd been dreading it all week. But at least it wasn't showstopper time yet. I had until tomorrow to conquer that doozy.

When Fiona yelled "action," Elspeth stepped forward.

She smiled at everyone, taking time to lock eyes with us one by one. Immediately, the gnawing thrum in my body began to calm.

"This week's technical challenge is a decadent French classic, the Paris-Brest. Commissioned in 1910 to commemorate a bicycle race between Paris and Brest, the cake was created by Parisian pastry chef Louis Durand. Nowadays, the legendary Paris-Brest can be found in all French patisseries. It's one of the most popular desserts in the country."

Jonathon joined her side. "And one of my personal favorites," he added.

Hmm. I was sure he'd said that about all our challenges. Maybe Jonathon just liked cake.

"It's a choux pastry," he continued, "twisted into a circular shape just like a bicycle wheel and then filled with a sumptuous mix of whipped cream and praline. But don't be fooled —this shouldn't be a heavy dessert. If our bakers get it right, the choux pastry will be light as air. This cake should melt in the mouth. This won't be easy, will it, Elspeth?"

Elspeth shook her head. "No, it certainly won't. But choux pastry is worth mastering. It's the basis for many delicious desserts—éclairs and cream puffs, to name just two. So it's a great skill for our bakers to have under their belts."

"Indeed. And here we're looking for a light and fluffy praline cream perfectly balanced with a rich, intense, whipped-cream center," Jonathon said.

I recalled the time I'd heard him memorizing his own cookbook. Some of his lines sounded familiar. Was he quoting himself again?

Arty gave a cheeky smile. "There's always pressure in *The Great British Baking Contest's* tent. Speaking of which... Your time starts...now."

Florence shot me a smile. "Good luck," I mouthed back, and then looked nervously down at my equipment. My trusty food processor, piping bag, star nozzle and silicone mat. An array of mixing bowls, the ingredients set out before me. Pastry of any kind was not my forte, so I'd practiced the tricky choux all week—maybe not as much as my Bundt cake, a decision which I was now seriously regretting.

Just like in the previous challenge, I closed my eyes for a second and imagined myself back in my own kitchen. I felt my heartbeat begin to calm and my breath steady. I even imagined Mildred watching with her critical eye as I weighed my flour and sifted some onto a sheet of baking parchment. Just like earlier, my hands seemed to take charge, leading the way. It was like they were smarter than my actual brain. But no time for ruminating. There were so many steps to this cake, and we were already pressed for time. I had to get cracking. I poured the water, milk, salt, and sugar in a pan, and as it began to slowly boil, I cut the butter into small chunks and added them to the mix.

When the butter melted, and the water was bubbling, I took the pan off the heat and tipped in the flour, beating it vigorously until a dough began to form. Everything was going well, and my earlier nerves had completely disappeared. Was it possible that I was actually enjoying myself?

I felt a sudden warmth.

"Good work there, Poppy," Elspeth said. "Keep beating that dough until the side of the pan is clean."

Ah, maybe that good feeling was more witchy godmother than choux.

I kept up my beating and smiled back at Elspeth. Having her at my side increased my sense of calm a hundredfold, even though the camera had followed her. I felt like I could do anything.

"Almost there," I replied. "And then I'll pop this dough back on the heat for another five minutes or so." I felt confident and in control. But then Arty joined us. I hoped he wasn't going to crack a joke at my expense.

"Good to see you showing that dough who's boss," he said. "If the baking doesn't work out, would you consider a career as a lion tamer? Or a snake charmer?"

I forced a smile. If only Arty knew exactly how many jobs I was doing right now: graphic designer, baker, witch, amateur detective—he'd probably suggest adding professional juggler to the mix.

Thankfully, Elspeth and Arty moved on to speak to Florence. While the dough cooled, I could have a thirty-second breather. Naturally, I wanted to steal a peek at how everyone else was getting on.

Florence had her head down low, focused on her dough. She was still mixing, watching the bowl with the same intensity as an eagle stalks its prey. This girl was determined to win. I could hear Arty trying to distract her with his silly comments, but her concentration stayed on the task at hand. She did, of course, manage to keep her TV show persona sparkling, impressing Elspeth with a bit of historical knowledge.

"Well, actually, this dessert is known for its energizing, high calorific content, which gave energy to the cyclists in the grueling 1200-kilometer route race," Florence was saying. "The organizer of the race allowed the riders to rest in stages, and they'd tuck into a Paris-Brest and then speed off on a sugar high. But if you ask me, I think the bakers need it more. Especially as our race is against the clock. I'd lick the bowl if there weren't so many cameras around."

She laughed her throaty chuckle.

"Perhaps you could get away with a lick of the spoon, my dear," Elspeth suggested. "Chef's perks and all."

But their sweet chitchat was interrupted by a distressed cry from Priscilla. I looked over at her workstation. She appeared to be having a nightmare.

"I've overcooked my dough," she wailed. "It's too hard."

The cameras zoomed in on her plight, but luckily Elspeth swept in to help.

"Don't worry, Priscilla. It happens to the best of us. I don't think you can salvage this dough, but if you're quick, you can start again."

Priscilla was on the verge of tears. She looked at Elspeth in alarm. "I don't... I don't have enough time to begin again from scratch."

"Deep breaths now. I believe in you. Have a sip of water, clear your head, and then go back to your dough."

Priscilla's chin was still wobbling, but I could see that Elspeth's soothing tone was working its magic. Wait—was Elspeth using actual magic? She warned me against using my powers on the show, but could some of her own be slipping through the net here?

Jonathon joined Elspeth's side. He looked stern but added his own reassurances and said that he would stay with Priscilla so that Elspeth could move on and check in with Daniel. A look flashed between them, but I couldn't read what it meant. Those two had a private language that perhaps only belonged to elder witches.

But it wasn't long before Arty interrupted Jonathon and Priscilla's one-to-one. "I thought you might need me to lighten the mood here," he said, pushing his long blond hair out of his eyes. "Let me tell you—it's taken every inch of willpower I have to get this far in the challenge without making a breast joke. I literally have seven lined up and ready to go right now."

At that, Priscilla laughed. She dabbed at her eyes, worrying about her mascara smudging, but Arty told her that she looked lovely. That seemed to do the trick. Priscilla got back to her mixing bowl and began again.

"And that's how you do it, Jonathon," Arty said.

Jonathon laughed good-naturedly.

"Now that I've got you," Arty said, "perhaps you could tell me a bit more about why this is such a tricky technical bake for our contestants?"

Jonathon looked nonplussed for a split second and then sprang into action. Was he still memorizing lines and trying to recite them? I couldn't understand why Jonathon would have such little faith in his own abilities.

"The final product may appear to look simple," Jonathon said, "but there are hurdles that each baker will have to over-come. The biggest challenge is that choux pastry. They'll have to be careful not to overheat it—as we've seen with poor Priscilla here—and to get the right consistency. Then it's a balancing act between the light praline cream and the more intense whipped cream. We'll be testing their piping skills, too. This cake could easily look messy, so we're after accuracy and attention to detail in the final presentation."

Well said, Jonathon.

But now my lovely calm feeling began to dissipate. Time to turn my attention back to my workstation. I cracked my eggs, lightly beat them, and then slowly began to add them to my dough, staring into its depths, willing it to transform into a smooth and glossy consistency.

Next up was the piping, which I thought I'd become pretty good at during all my wedding cake preparation. In one sweeping motion, I piped four thick rings onto the lined baking sheet, then lightly brushed the top of the choux with egg wash and added some flaked almonds. There was nothing for it now but to wish my pastry well and slide it into the ovens. I'd have to keep an eagle eye on the time, as in fifteen minutes, the temperature would need to reduce in order for the choux to rise and turn a perfect golden color. There was no time to rest on my laurels.

I barely noticed now when a camera came close as I opened the oven and slid my tray inside.

I started work on the praline center, melting the sugar until it turned into a caramel, and then adding roasted hazelnuts. I poured the mix onto my silicone sheet and then went to take out my choux.

I peered into the oven with one eye half closed, scared in case I'd messed up and my pastry hadn't risen.

"Don't worry, Pops. I've been keeping a close eye on these ovens, and your choux is looking choux-lightful."

It was all I could do not to jump. There was a cameraman headed my way, and, oh great, Gerry, the friendly baking ghost, had decided to make an appearance. With all these cameras around, I couldn't risk responding to him, of course, but I smiled in his direction, while simultaneously trying to give him a stern look. I just hoped the result didn't look like I was having a stroke. That was so not the look I was going for in front of millions of home viewers.

"It's okay, Pops, I'm not sticking around. Just wanted to mess with the electrician, but I can't find him. Who's in the lead? Want me to move their pastry so it falls on the floor? I'd do it for you. You know I would. Not to be a buzzkill, but you may need some ghostly intervention."

I shook my head, hoping the home viewer would think I'd decided the pastry wasn't ready to come out of the oven, when really I was telling Gerry to stay out of my business. I did not want to win because a fledgling poltergeist decided to help me.

"Okay. Don't come crying to me when you're packing to go home, lovey."

And thanks so much for the vote of confidence. I watched with relief as Gerry floated through the calico awning.

I gave it another minute and then took out the pastry. All I had to do now was get the filling right.

I blitzed the praline into a fine dust—this part was great for releasing tension—and then turned my attention to whipping the vanilla cream. With another piping bag ready, I sliced the choux in half, laid the praline on the bottom, piped some beautiful cream swirls, then sprinkled the remaining praline dust over the top and placed the other half of the choux on like a lid. It looked wonderful.

"Bakers, you have five minutes remaining," Jilly called out.

Wow. I'd been so in the zone, somehow I'd managed to finish early. The time had flown past. All my Paris-Brest needed now was a light dusting of icing sugar and then voila. Calorific pastry goodness, here I come.

I carefully plated up and stood back from my workstation. Exhaustion came over me in a sudden wave. I'd been riding the adrenaline for the past two hours and, now that I'd completed my task, I realized how drained I felt. I needed a good sit-down. But I knew I couldn't rest yet. There was still a nagging voice inside me, telling me to go back to the Orangery as soon as the judging was over. I was sure there was something I'd missed, and if my energy was actually tied up with the Cupid, then maybe I could do a quick hunt for it myself, simply to set my mind at ease. I needed to know that I'd done everything I possibly could to help solve this murder.

With a minute go, there was panic in the air. Like me, Maggie had finished. But Amara was piping her cream; Hamish was even further behind, still slicing his pastry in half. But I was most concerned for Priscilla, who hadn't even finished whipping her cream. There was no way she was going to be able to pull each element together in time. I ran over to help—she could do with an extra pair of hands right now. Florence was watching Priscilla, too. She caught my eye and mouthed, "Uh-oh." I couldn't tell if she was feeling sorry for Priscilla or gloating. But no matter how much she wanted to win, she couldn't be that cruel, surely?

"Looks fabulous," she said, gesturing at my bake. I glowed with pride. It did look wonderful!

"Same to you," I replied. Her layer of piped cream was much thicker than mine, and the resulting cake looked even more plump and inviting.

Maggie got to Priscilla at the same moment I did, and while Priscilla frantically piped her cream, we went behind her, putting the tops on and sprinkling icing sugar.

"Time's up, bakers," Arty called out. "Please bring your Paris-Brest to the judging table."

"Thanks, you two," Priscilla said in a mournful tone. I couldn't blame her. Because her cream hadn't been whipped long enough, it oozed out of the pastry. The very pale pastry, because she'd had to pull it out of the oven before it had browned.

Once the cakes were in a row, Elspeth took a step forward. "Congratulations, bakers. You've made it through this complicated round. You had a lot to do in very little time, and looking at what you've all produced, I have to say I'm very proud. You've come a long way, and we've not let up the pressure. I'm looking forward to tasting each of your bakes."

Elspeth was so lovely. I was so lucky that she was my witchy godmother.

Jonathon didn't let up the pressure, however. "We'll be looking for a satisfying crisp but light pastry, well-set cream, and a nice crunch from the layer of praline."

"Yes, it's the consistency of the cream that concerns me most," Elspeth added. "I don't want it sloppy, but I don't want it over-whipped either."

"A regular Goldilocks, our Elspeth," Jilly joked.

Everyone laughed, but it was that kind of laughter which sounded more like scared little lambs bleating.

"But in all seriousness," Jonathon added, "we'll be looking at the color and texture of your praline cream to see how proficiently you mixed your ingredients. We want to make sure it hasn't been overbeaten or if you've been too heavy-handed with nuts."

I waited with bated breath for Arty to make a joke about being too heavy-handed with nuts...but even Arty let this one go.

As always, the judging process was excruciating. I knew they were making comments about lightness, creaminess, and presentation, but I couldn't focus on the details. That is, until they got to mine. I held my breath and watched as they cut into my cake. Jonathon took a huge bite, Elspeth a more delicate mouthful. I studied every reaction that crossed their faces and then let out my breath as in unison they broke into smiles.

"Delicious," Jonathon said, his blue eyes wide and sparkling. "Creamy, nutty, intense but light, too."

"I agree," Elspeth said. "The choux pastry is light, with a lovely crunch. Excellent flavor. It's quite lovely."

I was so happy I hadn't disappointed. I'd done it! I'd managed to get through day one of baking without any trouble. Gone was the distracted, troubled Poppy of last week. The one who made silly mistakes, who couldn't keep her head in the game. I was back where I should be—working hard, pleasing the judges, and doing myself proud. I grinned.

And it turned out that almost everyone else had knocked it out of the park, too. Elspeth and Jonathon were bestowing praise to Maggie, Florence, and Hamish. Amara and Daniel had glowing reviews. Gaurav was praised, but Elspeth said his vanilla cream was too sweet. Jonathon added that he thought his choux was a little overdone.

But there was some heavy criticism for Priscilla.

"Priscilla, you had a bit of a wobble early on in the process. And I think you recovered remarkably. Time is tight for this challenge, so to start again from scratch was brave, and you did so well to get this far. But obviously your Paris-Brest isn't the best. The pastry is still wet in the middle. Obviously the cream's a bit wet, so it's not holding up the choux properly. The praline is very tasty, though." Elspeth spoke with a soft voice. I admired her gentle nature, how sensitive she was to people's feelings. She had none of Jonathon's abruptness. She could see how much this competition mattered to us. And she honored our dedication.

But despite Elspeth's words of encouragement, Priscilla turned bright pink. The poor woman. My heart went out to her. I wanted to tell her that all wasn't lost. I'd had a wobble last week, too, but I'd managed to stay in the competition. She could turn it around. As soon as filming was over, I'd go and give her a big hug.

The judges conferred, letting us squirm before giving their final verdict. I couldn't predict who might come in top place, though I didn't need my witch's intuition to guess who'd be on the bottom. You could hear a pin drop.

Then they were ready with their verdicts. I held my breath again, desperate for the judging to come to an end. I thought I would be safe. Priscilla was teetering on the edge, and there hadn't been as much praise for Gaurav, either, especially not considering his earlier triumph.

To no one's surprise, Priscilla was in last place. Then Daniel, then Gaurav. I was surprised to hear Maggie's name next, and then mine. Darn. I hadn't cracked the top three for a second time.

"In third place is Florence," Elspeth said.

We all clapped. She took a mini curtsy and beamed at the cameras.

Jonathon stepped forward. "And Hamish is our runner-up."

"Yay, Hamish!" I whispered, clapping him on the back.

"And the winner is—Amara!"

Wow! Now that is not what I expected at all. It only went to show that you couldn't predict who was going to come out winning. But I was thrilled for Amara. She'd kept her head down all competition, and now she was really coming into her own. We crowded round her and said our congratulations.

The cameras stopped rolling, and the group went back to their workstations for a final tidy-up before we'd be released back into the wild for another evening. But before I could begin to devise a good excuse for not following them to the inn, Robbie, the sound guy, came over. There'd been a problem with my sound when they'd filmed me mixing my dough.

"Could you pretend to be mixing and repeat what you said to Elspeth? I think it was something like, 'Almost there. And then I'll pop this dough back on the heat for another five minutes or so.'"

I cringed. Wasn't it bad enough that I sounded like a dork on camera without having to say it twice?

I agreed, of course, and stayed back while the others went to the inn to crack open a bottle of wine or two. At least this way I had a good excuse for being late to the party. A quick visit to the Orangery, and then I'd join them for a well-earned gin and tonic.

"Could I say something more interesting this time?" I begged Robbie.

He laughed. "Course you can. I won't tell."

I tried to think of something witty and pithy and ended up saying, "Almost there. And then I'll pop this dough back on the heat for another five minutes or so."

CHAPTER 11

I stepped out of the tent and into the cool early evening. The sun had moved behind the clouds, and I took gulps of fresh air. It wasn't until you came back into the real world that you realized how much your clothes smelled of butter and flour and vanilla. Which was a real bummer considering we had to keep the same outfit on for both days of filming to make it look like everything was shot in one day. As if mere mortals could actually bake that much in twenty-four hours.

I shivered in my shirtdress and cursed myself for always forgetting to bring a cardigan or light jacket.

I crossed the freshly mowed lawn, filling my lungs with crisp spring air. I never grew tired of roaming the grounds of Broomewode, admiring the immaculate gardens and Georgian architecture. But as much as I would have loved a leisurely stroll, maybe popping in on Susan Bentley and Sly to see how they were doing, my feet moved of their own accord in the direction of the Orangery.

As I walked, I heard a faint meow. I looked down, and there was Gateau, rubbing up against my ankles.

"Have you been staying out of trouble, little one?" I asked. "You'll be pleased to learn that your cat mom has finally redeemed herself on the baking front."

She tilted her head up and stared at me as if to say, *Oh, sorry, was I supposed to care about your silly competition?*

"Come on, some solidarity for Team Poppy, please," I said. "Not everyone's life can be all treats, snoozing and butterfly-chasing." Which seemed a shame. I bent down and took her into my arms. "But you can make yourself useful and be my trusty sidekick while we visit a murder scene. Elspeth said you're my partner, so now you have the perfect opportunity to put your familiar skills to the test. Right?"

I rubbed the spot between her eyes, and she purred.

Cat in arms, I felt a little bit braver. Something was amiss at the Orangery, and I was determined to get to the bottom of it.

As I followed the pebbled path away from Broomewode Hall, I kept thinking about the cupid statue. I'd only just discovered my power of telekinesis, but what if it was stronger than I knew? What if I really had been responsible in some way, dreaming about Stupid Cupid and moving it in my sleep? Just the thought was unbearable. Surely my powers couldn't be used for harm? That must be against the witch code—if there was one, that is. I suddenly felt hopeless. I knew so little about being a witch. What with searching for clues about my birth mom, the wedding, and the competition, I'd barely paid any attention to learning more about the coven. Elspeth's magic circle had helped me understand more about the sisterhood, but there was a long way to go. And if my powers were actually causing harm, I owed it to the universe to harness them for good. I had to make the time to study and grow. Not only did I owe it to myself, but I owed it to the people around me.

I quickened my pace and soon reached the Orangery. "Darn it," I said to Gateau, who lifted her head lazily and then put it straight back down again. The place was crawling with forensics. It was a million miles from the serene scene of Friday morning. The building itself hadn't changed, of course. The windows were still huge and gleaming, the wisteria still lovely. But the wedding arrangements looked so sad. The potted plants at either side of the entrance; the semi-circle of chairs arranged on the terrace; the rows of tall vases filled with beautiful pink and white flower arrangements to form an aisle. Saddest of all was the trellis arch, wound with white roses under which Lauren and Ryan should have said their vows.

Instead, there was the terrible static of walkie-talkies crackling through the air, and through the window, I could see people dressed in white jumpsuits. I guessed they were still searching inside for clues.

I didn't want to raise any suspicions, so I turned away from the Orangery and headed to the pretty stream that ran through the grounds. If I wanted to get back in touch with my witchy feelings, then what better place for a water witch than the stream? Maybe if I poured my focus into imagining a vision, then a clue to what happened here might appear on its surface.

Gateau wriggled in my arms, so I set her down. "Stay close, little one," I murmured. "You need to be my watch-cat."

I stopped by the ornate white bridge. Yesterday morning, it had seemed the perfect spot for staging wedding-day photographs; now it was just eerie and sad. But the bridge was a good spot for me to stand and peer into the water's depths. I was about to walk up when I saw a figure approaching it from the other side. It was probably someone from the investigation. I didn't want to be dragged into a conversation about why I was loitering near a murder scene, so I turned on my heels and followed a path away from the Orangery, toward the mouth of the stream, where I could take refuge behind some bushes until they left.

I looked around for Gateau, but she'd scampered off. Some familiar.

From my safe spot behind a bayberry bush, I realized it wasn't a police officer approaching the bridge. It was Lauren.

She was dressed in jeans and what looked to be a man's shirt. My heart stopped for a moment—was she wearing one of Ryan's shirts? That was too sad. She stopped halfway across the bridge and leaned over the railing. From my hiding place, I could see she was weeping. Poor Lauren. I couldn't stay here without at least trying to comfort her, but as I was about to straighten up, Edward, the gardener, appeared at her side. He must have seen her in the distance.

He approached Lauren with a sad smile and pulled a packet of tissues from his overalls. She took one, looking grateful, and they exchanged a few words, which I couldn't catch. After a minute, Edward lightly touched Lauren's shoulder, and they turned away and walked off in the direction of the inn, which was just in the nick of time, as my legs were getting cramps from crouching behind the bush.

I was about to try the bridge again when a flash of something in the water caught my eye. I went closer to the stream. What was that? A fish? A rock? There was definitely something bobbing about in there. I peered in again. The water was rippling, but the current couldn't be that strong. Could it be the cupid? I closed my eyes and focused on the image of the statue with every ounce of energy in my body. "Come on, you cheeky cherub," I murmured. "Show yourself."

Slowly, an electric buzzing worked its way from my toes up into my legs and my stomach. My fingers began to twitch. I opened my eyes, and whatever was in the stream began to bob up and down, water swirling madly around it. "Come on, come on." But if it was the cupid, it was refusing to budge. I held on to the electric force in my body and tried to think of what Elspeth would do if she were here. "A spell!" I said out loud. But the only spell I knew was one for protecting, not summoning. Could I string one together? Would that even work? If only I'd paid more attention in Poetry 101 at college.

I could feel my strength falling away from me. There was nothing for it but to try.

Cupid, come to me as bidden
Let me see what may be hidden.
Show yourself, if you are near,
Help solve the crime committed here.
So I will, so mote it be.

I opened my eyes. There was a strange gurgling sound coming from the water, and the cupid statue rose out of the water and settled onto the bank.

I looked at the dripping statue, amazed that such an

angelic thing had been used to cause such terrible damage. There wasn't any sign of blood, and the statue seemed to be still intact. But then wouldn't the stream wash away any blood? No doubt that's why the killer had heaved cupid into the stream. I knew better than to examine it myself; it would be up to the police to investigate further.

As it stared at me, I could have sworn there was reproach in the stone cherub's eyes. "I'm so sorry," I said, "But you mustn't follow me anymore."

I sighed, thinking of how the little trickster had toyed with me in the Orangery.

> Cupid dear, our bond I break,
> No ties of love for me shall you make
> So I will, so mote it be.

Cupid didn't move but I felt that if the little guy had replied, he'd have said, "Don't come crying to me when you end up old and alone. You had your chance."

I left the water's edge and went to find the closest constable. As I walked back toward the Orangery, I realized that bits of mown grass were stuck all over my sneakers. I quickly brushed them off, afraid that they'd mark the white canvas. I didn't want to show up to set tomorrow with grass stains.

I had to admit, when I went to find an officer, I was hoping to be greeted by Sgt. Lane. But there wasn't a familiar face to be seen.

I told a lovely constable named Elvin that I'd seen the statue at the mouth of the stream, and he thanked me before calling for his partner on his walkie-talkie and rushing off. I stood watching him for a moment with a strange mixture of envy and trepidation. I was envious that he'd be one step closer to finding out who committed this awful crime and nervous that somehow that culprit might have been me. I was still clearly connected to the statue. I'd managed to lift it out of the water, after all. I hoped I'd now broken that connection, but what about when Cupid and I had been bonded? Did my erratic powers extend to my subconscious? Could I have moved the cupid in my sleep?

I broke into a cold sweat. I shivered and hugged my arms to my body. I could feel the panic rising. I needed Elspeth. I decided to walk back to the inn and find her. If anyone could give me some answers about my powers, it was my witchy godmother.

I felt something knock against my feet, and there was Gateau, back for another scratch behind the ear now that all the drama was over. "Perfect timing, as always, little one," I said. Honestly, she really needed to hone her skills as sidekick.

Together we walked back to the inn, and my heart soared as the entrance came into view and there was Elspeth, elegantly perched on the edge of the stone wall. She'd changed out of her filming outfit and into a pair of navy slacks and a pale gray cashmere cardigan.

I put Gateau down and ran toward her. "Oh, Elspeth, you've no idea how glad I am to see you."

Elspeth looked relieved. She reached behind her and produced a neatly folded black cardigan. "Here, I thought you might be chilly."

Wow, Elspeth was really tuned in to my body clock. I took

the cardigan gratefully and slipped it over my shoulders. It smelled of her perfume, soft and floral.

"I sensed something was happening with you," Elspeth said. "Not danger, exactly, but turmoil."

I nodded and told her that I was fine. "But can we talk? I need to get something off my chest, and you might be the only person who can help me."

She nodded solemnly and patted the space beside her. "Sit. Everyone else is inside, resting or settling in for an early supper."

I wished I could rest. I didn't realize how exhausted I was until I took up the offer and sat down. My legs were so tired from all the standing, I felt like I'd run a marathon. My stirring arm ached. I'd been through the wringer today.

Elspeth reached over and touched my arm. "Tell me what's troubling you, Poppy. You look pale."

I smiled weakly and then told her everything. The whole story of the wedding cake commission, meeting the bridal party, being coaxed into the silly ritual with the cupid, how I'd discovered I had the power of telekinesis, the shots of tequila I didn't have with Harry, the groom's father, the tensions between the men, and then finding Ryan's body with his head bashed in. I spoke so quickly and with such emotion, I barely stopped for breath. It wasn't until I reached the real reason for my story that I faltered.

"But that isn't the worst of it. What if somehow my connection to the cupid caused Ryan's death? Maybe I dreamed about moving the statue in the night or my subconscious ran away with itself... I don't know." I paused again and realized I was wringing my hands. I placed my left palm on top of my right and held them in my lap. "I don't understand what my powers are or what they're capable of. I'm terrified, Elspeth, that somehow I'm drawing death to Broomewode. You told me that the village is an energy vortex that draws witches, right? But look what's happened here since I arrived. What if my energy is drawing death?"

I looked up at Elspeth, waiting for her to admonish me for being a bad witch. But instead, her eyes were full of kindness. "Oh, Poppy, it doesn't work that way. Just because you're new to your powers doesn't mean you might accidentally be responsible for murder. The recent deaths in Broomewode have been tragic, yes, but they had nothing to do with you."

She patted my hand. "You did not cause those deaths. You solved the mystery by discovering the culprits. You helped their loved ones find peace. You've been bringing *good* into Broomewode, not evil." Her gaze was level on mine and full of wisdom. "As for wielding a statue as a weapon in your sleep, I've never heard of any such thing. You need a tremendous amount of focus, conscious focus, to move objects."

"But the cupid moved without me telling it to after I rubbed its belly while one of the bridesmaids repeated a foolish rhyme."

"Mmm. Perhaps in the future you'll be more careful about 'foolish rhymes.' You must remember you're not like other women."

Right. I was beginning to get the point.

"However, the cupid may have danced around when you were in the Orangery—no doubt that was your topsy-turvy emotion causing the statue to move—but you couldn't have caused it to randomly attack a man while you were sleeping. You must look elsewhere for that young man's killer."

At Elspeth's words, I could feel my worry melting away. "Thank goodness I'm not responsible."

"Not for a death, no, but you are responsible for your performance in the tent this weekend. Concentrate on baking first." She stood and brushed the dust from her slacks. "Now, go inside, eat a scrumptious dinner, and then take a nice, soothing bath. And for goodness' sake, clean the grass off your sneakers before tomorrow's filming."

CHAPTER 12

*I*nside the pub, the bakers were crowded around our usual table. I hung back for a moment, watching the scene. Everyone was talking excitedly, two open bottles of red wine on the table, menus being passed from hand to hand. The handsome Greek man Florence enjoyed flirting with yesterday was behind the bar. Despite the tragic wedding party, the pub was packed full of Saturday night revelers, determined to unwind from the week with good food and friends. I could feel my spirits lifting, but I couldn't afford to relax. There was a murderer on the loose, and I was determined to discover their identity and bring them to justice.

Hamish saw me loitering and waved me over.

I joined the group, and Florence poured me a glass of wine. Amara, Gaurav, Maggie and Priscilla were discussing their sourdough recipes. Daniel was looking at his phone. From his rapt expression I bet he had a new video message from his kids.

"Where have you been?" Florence asked.

I told them about having to re-film my stirring and that I went to the Orangery to see if I could help in any way with the investigation. I took a sip of the rich, red wine, letting the liquid warm my belly.

"Speaking of which," Hamish said, "the police have been checking alibis with every member of the wedding party."

Florence raised an eyebrow. "That's harsh. Surely they're all in mourning? Defending themselves from the police will be the last thing they feel like doing."

Hamish shook his head. "Sadly, friends and family are the first point of call for murder suspects."

The Greek barman (Darius, as Florence reminded me) came to take an order. Florence fluffed up her reddish curls and, to my astonishment, started to converse with him in Greek. Gaurav looked across the table at me, equally surprised. "A talented girl, this one," he said. I agreed.

I quickly scanned the menu and went for a warm goat's cheese salad with roasted figs and balsamic glaze. A bit of crusty bread on the side, and I'd be refueled and ready for tomorrow's finale. Just the medicine Elspeth ordered.

After Darius and Florence finished flirting and he'd retreated to the bar, I let everyone know that the police found the cupid statue in the stream (obviously leaving out the part where I used my magical powers to lift it out of the water).

Hamish softly whistled through his teeth. "That's great news it's turned up. But the downside of finding it submerged in water is that'll make it difficult to collect much forensic evidence. Any fingerprints will have been washed away."

"Ah," I said, shaking my head. So much for my big find. I took another sip of wine. If only I could pretend none of this was happening and have a nice, normal, relaxing dinner and another glass of wine. What would that even feel like?

Darius returned with a basket of warm, crusty bread. It was nestled in a red gingham cloth that matched the candles on the table. I took a roll and sliced it in half. Warm steam rose into the air, and I slathered the soft, white dough with yellow butter. The table went silent for a moment, enjoying the simple delights of bread and butter. But this peaceful scene was shattered as some of the wedding party arrived at the bar, downcast and maudlin.

"Isn't that the best man?" Hamish asked, pointing at where Joe had slumped into a barstool.

I nodded.

"I wonder if the police will actually get anywhere with the wedding party," Daniel said. "They can't really believe it was one of them. Isn't it more likely to be a psycho killer or something?"

Florence did her best damsel-in-distress face. "I certainly hope not. Maybe we can help the police and check people's alibis? We're not the police. They'll talk to us."

Gaurav nodded. "I'd love to help in whatever way I can. Maybe my research skills could come in handy again."

I looked across the table, surprised at how everyone was on board. I guessed they were as concerned as I was about a murderer on the loose. And perhaps, like me, they had started to feel a part of the Broomewode community. We were connected to one another by more than a love of baking or the desire to win a competition. We were a family of sorts, oddballs maybe, but with a united wish to protect the people around us.

Florence pointed at Joe, who was staring into a pint of ale. "I'll take the best man. He's quite dishy, and he fancies me."

"You know he's married, right?" I said. "And to the matron of honor."

"I'm only going to talk to him. I'm not planning to keep him." As though he were a pet she was thinking of adopting.

"Go easy on him, Florence. He just lost his best friend."

She shook her pretty head, and her curls bounced from side to side. "He was chatting me up at breakfast this morning. I commented on his wedding ring, and he said it's coming off."

I scoffed. "He's lying," I said. "Why do men do that? He and his wife, Ryan and Lauren—the four of them were besties."

Florence gave a very Italian shrug, as if to say, *Don't be so provincial, Poppy.*

Darius arrived with our food, and everyone took a breather from talking about murder to tuck into dinner. Several had ordered tonight's special, chicken and tarragon pie. How they could face any kind of pastry right now was beyond my comprehension. Florence, ever the convivial Italian host, topped up our wine and ordered another bottle.

I took a bite of my goat's cheese salad. The cheese was warm and oozed in the center. It was a perfect match for the sticky figs, which had been roasted with honey, and the peppery bite of arugula. I took another piece of warm bread and spread the cheese on top. Perfect.

But I almost choked when Gerry appeared, doing a floating genie-style number right behind Maggie's head.

I glared at him, stifling a groan. Why, oh, why wouldn't Gerry just be a good little spirit and pass over? All the way

145

over. I had visions of a passing-over ceremony, Elspeth and I leading the ritual, Gerry walking through an open door into a bright white light.

And me slamming the door behind him and locking it.

Luckily Hamish brought me back down to earth. "So I do have a list of the suspects and their alibis thanks to a little insider knowledge from DI Hembly and our very own Poppy."

Gerry floated over to my side of the table. "Ooh, now this is much more interesting than moving wooden spoons and spatulas around the pub kitchen. I wonder who is the prime suspect."

If only I could tell Gerry to vamoose. I swear he talked to me in public on purpose just to see if I'd keep my cool. He crossed his legs midair and settled his cheek in his palm, listening in with exaggerated concentration.

"So the strongest suspect is the groomsman who owed Ryan money."

Gerry rolled his eyes. "If he means the dark-haired bloke in room seven, he was snoring all night," Gerry said.

I swiveled my head slightly, trying to encourage him to continue without anyone noticing—although I probably looked like I was having an unfortunate neck spasm.

"I went in the guy's room to see if I could mess with him, you know, but it was like standing on a train track at rush hour. I moved his water glass over his face and spilled a few drops, and he still didn't wake up. I'd have said he was sleeping like the dead but..."

Very interesting. But how to pass on this important piece of evidence? It's not like I could say it had come from one of the baking contestants—a dead baking contestant.

I missed what else Hamish said as I saw Lauren arrive at the pub, her brother at her side and Jessica right behind her. The poor girl looked sick. Pale-faced, eyes red-rimmed. Ryan's shirt swamped her, and she looked frail and very little. They joined Joe, and Jessica settled beside her husband. A little ways behind them were some of the bridesmaids, including Kaitlyn and Kelly, who began to cry at the sight of Lauren. The bridesmaids moved to a table, and I could see that Kaitlyn was trying to get the girls to eat. Lauren broke away from the group and went to hug Harry, who sat at a table alone, sad and lost. They talked briefly, and then Lauren left, heading in the direction of the bathroom, no doubt to dry her eyes.

Priscilla finished her final bite of chicken pie and gestured at Harry. "I'll go and talk to him."

"Is he suspected of killing his own son?" I asked, incredulous.

"No," Priscilla replied, rising from the table and sending me a reproving glance. "But he could use a friend. And after the way I've been baking today, so could I."

Hamish said, "That's lovely, Pris. And if he does happen to talk about last night, see what he has to say." If I'd asked her, I'd have had an earful, I could tell, but when Hamish asked, she said she'd do her best but wouldn't ask rude, intrusive questions. She didn't glance my way, but I felt chastised. I was kind of hurt. Maybe I sometimes asked slightly insensitive questions, but I did have a pretty good track record of catching murderers.

"How about you, Amara?" Hamish asked. "You game for a little detective work?" She still looked flushed with pride from her win today, and I wondered if she'd even been listening or if she'd been reliving that lovely moment when she'd won the Paris-Brest round.

"I'll go and comfort the bride," she said, with dignity. "I shan't snoop."

"Who'll take the bride's brother?" Hamish asked, then looked at me. "Poppy?"

"Why not?" He'd dropped some hints that he'd be keeping his eye on Ryan. He obviously had something against the groom, but was it a big enough grudge that it would get out of hand?

Hamish turned to Maggie. "How about it? I'm sure you're excellent at comforting, looking after all those grandkids of yours."

It was fascinating watching Hamish kick into police mode. He was so good at rallying the group. If he worked my beat, I'd feel super safe at all times.

Maggie shook her head, readjusting her glasses. "I'm too old for sleuthing. I'm going to rest up for tomorrow. It's all right for you young people, but my feet are killing me after standing on them all day. A soak in the tub and a film on the telly. That's what I'll be doing."

"I understand," Hamish said. "Daniel? What about—"

But the dentist shook his head. "I need to call home. Talk to the kids."

"Of course," Hamish said, looking disappointed.

Darius returned to clear our empty plates, and Florence said something to him in Greek. It was obviously extremely amusing because he broke into a loud laugh that had all the elegance of a foghorn.

I turned to Gaurav. "Will you chat to a bridesmaid?"

"With pleasure," he said, and the normally shy Gaurav

had a gleam in his eye. I suspected he already had one picked out.

"What about you?" Florence asked Hamish.

"I'll take Jessica, the matron of honor. Let's see whether she thinks her marriage is over too, though of course they both have an alibi."

"What is it?" I asked.

Hamish moved the empty wineglasses to one side and leaned closer to the table. "According to the statement Joe gave the police, he arrived around midnight last night and went straight to bed. His wife confirms it."

I nodded. "That's true. Their room is next to mine. I heard him and Jessica talking. Well, more like Jessica talking at him."

Gerry coughed loudly. "He's lying. When I went snooping in their room, the woman was alone in bed."

I was so shocked I turned to him. "Are you sure?"

Gaurav, sitting on the other side of Gerry, looked startled. "Am I sure about what?"

I swallowed. "Well, are you sure you want to question the bridesmaid? Everyone will understand if you want to call it a night. We've a big day tomorrow."

He stood. "I am very sure. If you will excuse me."

I hoped I hadn't offended Gaurav. I thought his shyness was a charming quality, but maybe I'd embarrassed him by asking him if he wanted to speak to a pretty lady twice. Darn Gerry.

Hamish and Florence followed Gaurav's lead and dispersed to speak to their respective wedding guests. But before I could talk to Lauren's brother, I needed more info from Gerry. I told the others that I had to run upstairs to open the bedroom window for Gateau and that I'd be right back.

Fortunately, Gerry got the hint without me having to motion to him or otherwise make foolish gestures to what would look like empty air. He followed me out of the pub and up the stairs.

"Isn't this nice," he said, "us working together to try and solve another Broomewode crime."

I had to admit that Gerry had a unique set of sleuthing qualities. As well as being nosy and bored, he possessed another key skill—invisibility. Not even my witchy instincts could match that.

I opened my bedroom door and Gerry followed cautiously, looking around for Gateau.

"Don't worry," I said, "she's not here. Although I don't know what you're afraid of—she's just a harmless kitty. You're a ghost. That's way more terrifying."

Gerry did an approximation of a shudder. "She creeps me out."

Now that we were alone and free to talk without me looking like a madwoman, I asked Gerry to tell me everything he'd seen last night when he went to snoop on Jessica and Joe.

"Well, it was a restless night for me, Pops. I stuck my head in around one in the morning. Jessica was alone. And then about five a.m., I went back, still prowling, on the lookout for some decent entertainment, and Joe was there. They were sleeping as far away from one another as two people in one bed could manage. He was so far over on his side of the bed that his bare feet stuck out. I tickled them for fun, and he jumped up in bed and shouted. She turned her head and told him to shut up. Doesn't bode well, does it?"

But I wasn't so interested in the nuances of their sleeping habits. "I don't understand," I said. "I definitely heard Jessica talking to a man. If it wasn't her husband, who was it?"

Gerry and I stared at each other and at the same time said, "Ryan?"

CHAPTER 13

I was buzzing with questions about Jessica and Ryan. Why would a man who was getting married the next day be in another woman's room late at night? Maybe Gerry and I were jumping to conclusions about Ryan, but my gut was telling me we were right. And if I'd learned anything the past few weeks, it was to trust my intuition, even if it led me to uncomfortable conclusions. I guess I was also learning a lot about love, its strange trials and tribulations. I'd encountered so many couples keeping secrets from each other or the wider world—perhaps even from themselves.

Could Ryan have had last-minute wedding business to talk over with Jessica? They were all good friends. Maybe he wanted companionship the night before the big day.

And yet she'd sounded angry. I'd thought there was an argument going on next door. How I wish I'd been nosy then instead of tuning out the voices and going to sleep. Ryan and Lauren never got the chance to begin their next happy chapter. Love seemed to be full of strife and hardship. I should have thought twice about rubbing the cupid's belly and wishing for a handsome stranger to sweep me off my feet. I was better off with my sisterhood.

Gerry looked at me. "You still there, Pops? You were miles away. Do we think we're jumping to conclusions?"

"What conclusions? We don't have any. There's Julius, who seemed to owe Ryan money. The bride's brother, who seemed to have a grudge against the groom. Now we have the possibility that Jessica was telling Ryan off the night before he got married. Why? Had she heard rumors too? Maybe she was telling him to get his act together or she'd tell her best friend what he'd been up to."

"It's possible. But now Joe is talking divorce. What do you bet he arrived earlier than expected and caught Ryan and Jessica together?"

My eyes widened at yet another possibility. "You think he assumed they were having an affair and killed Ryan in a jealous rage?"

Gerry nodded, but then I remembered that if that were the case, I would have heard something through the door. Shouting or a scuffle.

I said as much to Gerry, who looked dejected. "Good point."

He soon rallied. "Or how about this: Joe opened the door to the room and saw them, but they didn't see him. Or else he saw Ryan coming out of his wife's room. The night before his wedding, too, and he snapped. So Joe followed him to the Orangery or lured him there somehow. Killed him with Cupid, symbol of romantic love."

"It's possible, I suppose," I said. "But the four of them were best friends. Wouldn't they have had a brawl? Maybe Joe would have punched his friend up a bit, but kill him?"

Gerry spread his hands wide. "What do we know about him? Why did he come down after everyone else?"

"Yes. And now that you mention it, Jessica said she and Ryan drove down together. But she mentioned it right in front of Lauren, which she'd hardly do if she was guilty, would she?"

"Don't ask me. I never understood women when I was alive. They aren't less mysterious now. I'm nothing but a snooping spirit."

"I'm about to talk to George, the brother. I'll see what he knows."

"Be careful, Pops. The brother had motive too. Cupid likes to shoot arrows into people. Bashing them over the head is human."

I smiled. It was sweet when Gerry looked out for me. "While I'm doing that, you go check both their rooms."

Gerry somersaulted in the air. "Ooh, goody. What for?"

I showed Gerry my sneakers. "You're looking for flecks of grass on the bottom of their trousers and on their shoes."

He looked at me blankly. "Pops, that means nothing. Why are you suddenly concerned about their levels of cleanliness? Maybe the pressure's getting to you."

I laughed, although I was exhausted and could probably have done with an early night, not a sleuthing session. But the truth had to come out. For so many people's sakes.

"You've got to trust me," I said to Gerry. "It means everything. Yesterday, the gardener mowed the area around the Orangery, but he only raked where the wedding guests would be. The area near the stream was never raked. So anyone with bits of grass stuck to their trousers would have been near the stream."

"Excellent deduction, Holmes. Watson's on the case. You can count on me." He tried to high-five me (he still wasn't completely au fait with the whole ghost thing) and then disappeared through the wall.

I splashed my face with water, combed back the flyaways that had finally escaped Gina's expert ponytail, applied a slick of gloss to my lips, and then followed up on Elspeth's advice to clean up my sneakers. I slipped them off and brushed off the bits of grass still stuck to the sides and bottoms. A small grass stain remained, but I couldn't do anything about that now. Besides, if my hunch was right, I'd have to be thankful for those stains—they might just be my biggest clue toward solving the mystery of Ryan's murder.

Downstairs, Team Baking Show had dispersed and was doing me proud. Florence was in the corner with Joe, resting her pretty head on her hands and batting her eyelashes. Next to them, Priscilla and Harry looked to be deep in conversation, talking in hushed tones, and Amara was by Lauren's side, holding her hand as she silently wept. I was in awe of their generosity, how much they were willing to come together and help the community. I really cared about these bakers. Then I chuckled inwardly. My bakers' street irregulars.

Hamish was sitting at a table with Jessica and another bridesmaid. Ever the professional, he'd arranged the table so that he could also keep an eye on how Joe was responding to Florence's advances and make sure that Jessica couldn't see what her husband was up to either. *Smart thinking, Hamish.*

I looked back at Florence again. She'd scooted her chair even closer to Joe's. I was worried she was getting into character a little too much. After Gerry's revelation, Joe was now a solid suspect. I had to warn Florence that dishy or not, Joe could be a cold-blooded killer. I caught her eye and made a sign for her to follow me to the bathrooms.

With an audible sigh, she excused herself and met me in the pub's restroom. It was actually a lovely room, decorated with pretty palm-leaf wallpaper, shell-shaped uplights and the same heavenly-smelling prickly pear and bramble hand soap as our bedrooms.

Florence went straight to the mirror and fluffed up her hair. "What's the matter, Pops? I was really reeling Joe in there. I mean, I'd barely even got started on my playbook of tricks, you know, eye-batting, complimenting, feigning interest in his favorite sport, and he was lapping up the attention."

I raised an eyebrow. Is that what it took to attract a man? Pretending to care about golf? No thanks.

"Exactly," I said. "I need you to be careful. Joe is now our leading suspect." I explained my theory about Ryan and Jessica.

"Goodness me," she said, shaking her head. "But really, Pops, I think he's far too handsome to be a killer. And he hasn't let anything slip about his wife yet. In fact, I don't think he's even mentioned her. The English are so pedantic about matters of the heart."

"I don't think it works like that," I said.

Florence shrugged but agreed to stay in the pub, where she was surrounded by friends and it was safe.

I left Florence reapplying her eyeliner and went in search of Lauren's brother.

I found him propping up the bar, half-cut and talking to a clearly bored Darius about his motorcycle.

I took the seat next to him and ordered a small glass of red. I was going to need to keep my wits about me this evening.

Darius handed me the drink with a look that said, *Please save me from this rambling fool.* Happy to oblige, Darius.

"It's George, right?" I said, swiveling on my barstool to face him. He was wearing the same outfit as last night—white T-shirt and jeans—although I was sure it was a different white T-shirt. Sort of like what we did on the baking show when we bought duplicates to wear on Sunday so the show would have a seamless look to it, as though all that baking and judging happened in one long session.

George looked blankly at me as though he'd never seen me before. So good for my ego. I bet he'd have remembered Florence if he'd met her instead of me. I tried to look enthusiastic about seeing him again. "We met in here last night. I'm the baker, Poppy Wilkinson."

"Ah, the ill-fated cake maker," he said, slurring his words a little, "for the wedding that would never happen."

I swallowed some red wine. True, yes, but it sounded even more horrible hearing someone else say it out loud. I told him how sorry I was about Ryan.

"Terrible, terrible," he muttered. "An awful betrayal." I felt my eyes widen. Was he saying what I thought he was saying? Did he know something?

"I don't understand," I said, although I was sure I did.

"My sister. She doesn't deserve this." He looked over to where Lauren was sitting quietly with tears running down her face. "No, she doesn't."

"No one deserves to lose their husband-to-be the night before their wedding."

He jerked his body toward me. "You think that's—" But before he could finish the sentence, he'd hit his drink with his elbow and knocked it over. I jumped out of the way as sticky rum and Coke spilled over the bar top and dripped down the edge. Darius sighed and grabbed a cloth while George stared at the mess as though someone else had done it.

I wished George wasn't so drunk. Though maybe his condition would make him more likely to share what he knew with a stranger. I was figuring out the right way to ask more questions when I spotted Sgt. Lane through the window, about to enter the inn. He looked tired. He'd probably been working flat out since yesterday morning. I quickly excused myself (not that George noticed) and went to intercept Sgt. Lane before he came into the pub.

I rushed to the entrance and caught him. He looked at me in surprise.

"Hi," I said, dumbly.

"Poppy. Is everything all right?"

"I wanted to speak with you privately."

He smiled, and the faint lines around his tired eyes crinkled. And those dimples, oh boy. "Does this have anything to do with the famous Poppy Wilkinson hunch?"

So long as no one guessed I was a witch, I was happy to be credited with great hunches. "I do have a theory, yes. A strong one, in fact. The bakers and the wedding party have been talking." Even though we were alone, I lowered my voice to a whisper. "I think you should take a close look at Joe."

He looked surprised—so not the look I was going for. "The best man? The dead man's closest friend?"

He did not seem enamored of my hunch, but I nodded anyway.

He looked past me into the pub, where most of the wedding party and some of the guests were congregated. Not in a happy way. "We have a warrant to arrest one of the groomsmen."

"Julius?"

"Yes, that's him. This is confidential, of course, but since I suspect you know this already, we discovered that he owed Ryan a lot of money."

I nodded. "And Ryan wanted it back."

"Exactly. Except he was never going to get it. After the wedding, Julius had a one-way ticket to Argentina booked. His business was bankrupt."

I paused before replying, trying to arrange this new detail in my mind. It did make Julius seem like a more shady character. But it didn't quite add up to him being the murderer. If he had zero intention of paying his friend back and was going to disappear to Argentina after the wedding anyway, why bother to murder the poor guy? Unless Ryan had found out...

"I see why he's your prime suspect," I said. "But there's something about Joe that I don't like. The way he talks about Jessica. And the way he talks about Ryan, too. There's disdain in his voice. If he believes his best friend and his wife were having an affair, surely that's some serious motive for murder? Crime of passion."

"But you said yourself you heard them talking in the room next door to you, and Jessica confirms he was with her all night."

I could hardly tell a police officer that I was getting information from a ghost.

159

"I heard a man and a woman talking in the room next door. I assumed it was Joe, but I can only confirm that it was a man. What if it was Ryan in her room?"

"That's a lot of 'what if,' Poppy. Where's your proof that they were having an affair?" he asked. "So far, it's just a bit of gossip. We need something more concrete."

So much for him believing in my hunches. Still, he was right. I needed hard evidence. But how? It wasn't like I could call on Gerry as a witness.

Sgt. Lane yawned. "Excuse me," he said, covering his mouth with his hand. "It's been a long twenty-four hours."

I said he should get some dinner in the pub. It wasn't like Julius would be going to Argentina tonight. He was sitting with a pint, talking to Kelly, clearly with no idea that he was soon to be arrested.

"You're right," he said. "Can't remember when I last ate a hot meal."

"You need to keep your strength up if you're going to track down a murderer," I said.

Oh no, was I starting to sound like his mom?

Together, we walked back into the pub. George was still drunkenly rambling to Darius. The rest of the baking gang had mingled nicely with the wedding party. Let the gossip flow.

"The bakers seem rather friendly with the wedding party and guests," Sgt. Lane said, following my gaze. Did he suspect Hamish and I had put them up to it? He was a detective, after all.

I only said, "I think most of the people here could really use a friendly shoulder to cry on."

I told Sgt. Lane he should find himself a quiet table and order something for dinner.

"Have you eaten?" he asked.

For a moment, I couldn't remember if I had or not. Was he asking me to join him? Or simply being polite?

"Yes, with the other bakers after filming ended. It's hungry work."

Great chat, Pops.

"Ahem." I spun round. It was Gerry. Great. When I was trying to look like a professional in front of a sharp-eyed detective, I did not need to be waylaid by a chatty ghost.

"I've been looking for you," he said.

I tried to pretend he wasn't there.

"But turns out you have more pressing matters to attend to." He gestured at Sgt. Lane, who was poring over a dinner menu and looking like he wanted to order it all.

I walked away, knowing he'd follow, and found a quiet corner. "What is it?"

"I popped into the snoring bloke's room earlier."

"Julius? The groomsman who borrowed money from Ryan?"

"The one over there talking to the pretty bridesmaid."

"Right, that's Julius."

"He was on his phone talking to a travel agent about rebooking a flight."

Here I was trying to prove Julius hadn't killed Ryan and he was doing everything he could to act guilty.

Was I wrong?

CHAPTER 14

*I*f I was to prove that Julius wasn't the killer, I didn't have long to do it. Were they planning to arrest Julius tonight? I had no idea, but I felt that time was running out. Sgt. Lane looked like he was getting ready to go up to the bar and order his food. I hoped he was a slow eater.

To my delight, Eve appeared behind the bar. I rushed over and asked where she'd been.

"Helping out the kitchen this evening," she said. "They were a man down."

A man down was exactly my problem, too. I told her about my hunch and asked if she'd help buy me a little more time to prove it. "He won't be able to go after the wrong person until he's eaten," I said. "So perhaps his order could take a little longer than usual..."

Eve gave me a long-suffering look. "Do we really have to have another dramatic incident in the pub? You'll give the place a bad name." However, she reluctantly agreed.

I caught Hamish's eye and gestured for him to round up the other bakers. We needed to debrief. And fast.

One by one, we returned to our usual table. Everyone looked very serious until Florence giggled. "This is just like a method acting class I took once, where we all had to go to a pub and pretend to be trees and then discuss people's reactions in the group afterward." I guess our expressions said it all because then she said, "Well, anyway, you had to be there. But I did manage to confirm that Joe is planning to divorce Jessica."

"Because...?"

She tossed her head. "Apart from the fact that I told him I don't date married men, he's convinced she's been cheating on him."

"With...?" I pressed.

"He wasn't on the witness stand with his hand on a Bible, Poppy. I was being a sympathetic ear, remember. He muttered something about not speaking ill of the dead. That's as close as I got."

Darn it. Sgt. Lane couldn't arrest a man because Florence had heard him refuse to speak ill of the murdered man. Bit of a dead end, though Florence might get a date out of it. Probably a date with a murderer.

Priscilla and Amara both drew a deep breath. "You think the groom was cheating on his wife before she even got married?" Priscilla asked in horror.

"And with her best friend?" Amara added.

There was still part of me that was shocked, too. I'd really bought into the story about Jessica and Lauren's friendship and their perfect love stories.

I looked at Hamish. "Did you get anything from Jessica?" He was an actual cop. I bet he was good at interrogating people and being subtle about it.

He took his time answering, and we all waited. Maybe not with bated breath, but he definitely had all our attention. "Well, Jessica is certainly upset about something," he said. "She was very skittish when we spoke. It could be that she was recovering from Joe's news. Or anticipating it." He tapped his fisted hand up and down against his thigh, as I'd seen him do when he was thinking. "Does she believe her husband's about to divorce her, or does she think he murdered his best friend?"

"Perhaps she's terribly upset that her friend, and possibly her lover, has been brutally killed," Amara reminded us. She was right. The murder alone could make her act squirrelly.

"How about Harry?" I asked Priscilla. I'd watched them talking together. I'd even heard Harry's laugh, once. Not the usual booming, hearty laugh that made people look up and want to join in, but a single crack of laughter, as though he'd recalled something funny. Then it was quickly silenced.

"He's devastated, as you can imagine that such an awful thing happened to his son. Poor man."

"Did he have any idea why it happened?"

"No. He only kept saying that now he was glad his wife was gone so she'd never have to live through such a terrible thing. He believes it was a robbery gone wrong. That Ryan probably went for a walk, maybe with pre-wedding nerves, and surprised a burglar."

"So he doesn't blame anyone here?"

She looked like she might cry. "He blames himself. He says he should have been walking with his son. He feels he let him down."

"Oh, that's so sad," Amara said.

"In fact, I should get back to him. He shouldn't be alone at a time like this. I told him I'd get him a brandy."

We watched Priscilla walk over to the bar. Was she being a good citizen, or had Harry won her affections even in his grief? Either way, I was glad Priscilla could offer some comfort. It was heartbreaking to see Harry, once so gregarious, now in so much pain.

Amara spoke next. "Lauren is in shock. It will take her a while to process what's happened. But from the sounds of it, she's got a good family, and they'll support her through this. She promised me that she'd see her family doctor, but in the meantime, I've offered her some herbal sleeping pills so that she can rest tonight."

"That's kind of you." I'd almost forgotten that in her real life, Amara was a doctor. It was so easy to think that baking was all any of us did. But now I could see Amara's kind bedside manner, her years of experience.

"Did she say anything that might help identify her groom's killer?"

"No. She seemed like a woman completely in love. She said he loved her and she loved him, and she began to tell me of their plans. They were to look at a house next week. She was very excited about that. Said it was at the top of their budget but exactly what they'd been dreaming of."

"Which was why Ryan was so anxious to get his loan paid back by Julius," Hamish muttered. He glanced at me. "You sure it wasn't him who did it? The police like him for it, I can tell you."

I was beginning to doubt my own hunch. But again, Gerry had haunted Julius's room and found him snoring. I couldn't tell them that. I was beginning to wonder if Gerry could be trusted. Was he toying with me the way he played tricks on the hotel guests?

"Maybe, but I'm not convinced," I said.

Gaurav spoke as though he couldn't be silent any longer. "Kaitlyn didn't seem to know much about her friends' relationships. But she did agree to go on a date with me." He looked extremely pleased with himself.

"Go, Gaurav," Hamish said.

"That's wonderful," I said. We all began to congratulate him as though he'd been named the episode's Best Baker.

I recalled the foolish ceremony where we single women had rubbed Cupid's stone belly. At least Kaitlyn's wish for a good man might come true. Maybe something good could emerge from this tragedy.

They turned to me, then. "George was drunk and rambling," I said. "I know he distrusted Ryan, but I didn't get much sense out of him."

"Well, bakers, we've done what we could," Hamish said. "But we should really be getting an early night. We've the showstopper tomorrow."

Priscilla came toward us, presumably on the way to the bathroom. Hamish said, "Don't get so carried away with Harry that you forget you've got a big day tomorrow, Pris."

"Don't remind me," Priscilla groaned, stopping and putting a hand to her head. "I can't do anything right. I feel like my only chance tomorrow is to reverse everything. See if I can surprise the judges into a good result. I'll flip everything on its side. What should taste sweet is bitter, what should be sour is sweet. White is black and black is white." She was joking, but I found myself with my mouth wide open. Of course. I'd been looking at this backward.

166

I looked over at Sgt. Lane. DI Hembly had joined him, and the pair of them were chomping through steak and chips at an alarming rate.

Hamish stood up, and that was the cue for all of us to head up to bed.

I'd thought I had things clear in my head, but now I realized I'd been completely wrong. Or at least, that's what my gut was telling me now.

"Wait!" I said, and everyone turned to stare at me.

"Florence, one quick question. Do you remember what Jessica was wearing last night?"

If anyone would, it was Florence and her Italian eye for fashion.

"Of course. She looked fabulous. It was a gorgeous cream silk two-piece: a beautifully cut camisole with a matching pair of wide-legged silk trousers. Also cream. Not everyone can pull that kind of thing off, but she did it wonderfully. Why do you want to know?"

"Just something I was thinking about," I said.

Florence put a hand on my arm and shook her head. "No, Poppy. That look's not for you. You're more girl-next-door. Comfort over style. You do very well in your jeans and your casual shirts. But a cream silk two-piece?" She closed her eyes briefly as though the vision of me looking sophisticated was too much. "No, *cara mia*. No."

And thanks for that.

No one argued with her. It wasn't that I didn't know my fashion limitations, but I felt like she was telling me I was born dowdy and would die dowdy.

"Guys, can you wait around for a bit? I might need you."

Hamish narrowed his eyes at me. "What new hunch are you following?"

"Can't tell you yet. I could be wrong. But if I'm not..."

Hamish settled back. "I suppose a nightcap wouldn't hurt."

Once he sat down again, the rest followed.

I ran back upstairs in the hopes of finding Gerry. Luckily, he was floating down one of the corridors.

"Pops, that cat of yours has a bad attitude. She hissed at me." He looked horrified, though I didn't know why. It wasn't like Gateau could do him any harm. I suspected he was miffed that my familiar didn't like him. Even in life, Gerry had been an acquired taste.

"You're exactly the man I want to see," I told him, which perked him up. "I need you to search for something in Jessica's room. See if you can find a pair of cream silk trousers."

"Sounds kinky."

I had to laugh. "Just find them and tell me where they are. I need to go back downstairs."

"I'm on it, boss," he said, giving me a mock salute.

After Gerry left, I glanced out the window at the moon. The sky had turned dusky pink, and the moon was showing her face. I touched the purple amethyst necklace around my neck. If my gut was right, the next thirty minutes could be full of danger. I thought of Elspeth's protection spell and modified it to suit my purpose.

Earth, Fire, Water, all three,
Elements of Astral, I summon thee,
By the moon's light
I call to thee to give me your might

> *By the power of three*
> *I conjure thee*
> *To protect the innocent*
> *And the killer to see*
> *So I will, so mote it be."*

I touched the amethyst again for good luck and then legged it down the stairs.

Back in the pub, I wanted to speak to George again and find out exactly what he knew.

By the looks of it, George had just had his drink refreshed. I needed answers before he was too sozzled to speak.

I sat beside him, and he looked up, bleary-eyed. "Oh, it's you. You're back."

"I need your help, George. It's important you tell me the truth." I glanced around and then lowered my voice. "Were Ryan and Jessica having an affair?"

His eyes opened so wide, they actually looked white again. "I thought you were the cake-maker. What's all this about?"

"There's no time to explain. Were they?"

George took a sip of his drink. I glanced over at Sgt. Lane. He was munching on one of the last chips on his plate. Hembly had pushed aside his empty plate.

George sighed and looked dejected. "Yes. They were having an affair. Poor Lauren. She'd already come down here and was staying with Mum, getting things ready for the wedding. She asked me to drop by Ryan's place and drop off a bit of her wedding ribbon so he could make sure his bow tie matched."

He took another sip of his drink as though his throat was

dry. "When I got there, I saw Jessica standing at his front door. Didn't think much of it. Thought Lauren probably had her running errands as well. Then, as I was about to get out of my car, I saw Ryan was in bare feet and a bathrobe. They kissed."

"Could it be two friends kissing?" I didn't want to falsely accuse anyone.

He made a derisive sound. "No. I was fumbling with my phone, trying to get the camera on, and then she pushed him back inside the house, still kissing, and slammed the door."

Oh, that did seem suspicious.

"What did you do?"

He scowled at the bar. "What I should have done was banged on the door and punched him. But I didn't. I drove away."

"You were in shock," I said.

"Probably. Didn't know what to do."

"What did you do?"

"I called Lauren. I was going to tell her. Should have told her."

"But you didn't."

He shook his head. "How could I? She was so happy. She thought he was perfect. And she chattered away about the plans they had. The house, the baby, the future. She had it all planned out. I couldn't tell her," he admitted.

"Did you tell anyone?"

He started to push off his stool. "I need to go. Don't feel well."

I grabbed his arm. "George. You have to tell me. Who did you tell? I saw you come in here the night of the rehearsal. You were dropping some pretty broad hints."

"I went to him. Ryan. Before the dinner." His eyes burned into mine. "Told him I was going to tell my sister what I'd seen if he didn't break it off with Jessica. Ryan begged me not to say anything to Lauren. Said he'd already decided he was going to break up with Jessica that very night."

"What about Joe? Did you tell him?"

"He wasn't there. Now I have to go."

I didn't let go of his arm. "That's not an answer."

He screwed up his face like a man in pain. "I think I drunk-dialed him."

I held out my hand. "Show me your mobile." I was really getting into the mom thing tonight. Telling Sgt. Lane to eat his dinner, making George show me his phone. Well, according to Florence, seemed I dressed like a mom, so I might as well act like one.

As though I really were his mother, George pulled out his phone, unlocked it with his fingerprint and handed it over. I scanned through his calls. There it was. Just after ten last night, he'd called Joe, and the call had lasted two minutes and seventeen seconds. "You don't remember the call?"

"No. I must have told him." He sank back onto his barstool. "And then he killed Ryan. And now look at my poor sister. I wish I'd never seen Ryan and Jessica going at it. Then Ryan would still be alive and Lauren would be happily married." He buried his head in his hands. "It's all my fault."

"No. It's not. You tried to do the right thing."

He looked up, eager. "Really?"

"Yes." I asked Darius for water and pushed George's drink away. I was really on a roll with the mom thing. "George, I need you to sober up in case you have to repeat what you told me to the police. Can you do that?"

He nodded.

I looked around. Where was Gerry? I needed those trousers yesterday. Sgt. Lane was finishing his last few chips. If only Eve wasn't in the kitchen, then I could ask her to slow him down somehow. I'd have to ask Darius instead.

I caught his attention and tried not to be embarrassed by what I was about to do.

"What can I get you?" he asked with a smile.

"Actually, it's not so much what you can get for me..." I swallowed. "I have a favor to ask. Would you send Sgt. Lane and DI Hembly over there a dessert when they've finished their steak and chips? You can choose what, and put it on my room bill. The only thing is, I don't want them to know who bought it. It has to stay secret." I tried to channel my inner Florence and smile charmingly. "Completely secret."

Darius winked. "Very sly, I like it. The young one's dishy, isn't he? I'll order a chocolate fondant now—they take fifteen minutes to bake, but it's worth it."

"Perfect, thank you! Tell them it's coming and don't let them leave."

I ran up the stairs to find Gerry.

I found him sitting on my bed looking morose. He was empty-handed.

"Where are the trousers?" I asked.

He shook his head. "They're not there."

"But they have to be."

"Believe me, I've become a world-class snooper in the past few weeks. I looked everywhere in her room. Wardrobe, dresser, bathroom floor, under the bed. No trousers."

My heart sank. If they weren't in her room, where were they? What would a woman do with grass-stained trousers?

"The laundry!" I half-shouted, slapping my palm against my forehead. "Florence uses it all the time. You put soiled clothes out for pickup, and they're returned clean the next day. I only hope we're not too late."

"The machines are in the basement. I'll show you."

I followed Gerry to the ground floor and then down another set to the basement and an unmarked door. But the door wouldn't open. I pushed against it and tried the handle again. No luck. It was locked.

I turned to Gerry in despair.

He shrugged. "Don't look at me, Pops. I usually float through doors."

"Okay, you go in and get a head start looking for those trousers. I'll see if I can find Eve and get the door unlocked. Even if you find them, there's no way I can take them without explaining how I got through a locked door."

Gerry saluted me, and I ran back upstairs.

I arrived at the bar, gasping for air. Eve was at Sgt. Lane's table. He and DI Hembly were eagerly tucking into the chocolate dessert. I rushed over.

"Eve, I need the key to the laundry room."

The two detectives looked up.

"The laundry? Whatever for?" Eve asked. "If you've something that needs washing—"

"No. It's about the murder. I have an idea. Trust me. It's important. We need to go now."

My antics had attracted the attention of most of the room, and now the bakers came over.

Eve took a huge set of keys on a chain from her back pocket. "It's one of these. Let's go."

Sgt. Lane put down his spoon. "I'm coming with." I didn't

have the heart to tell him there was an adorable smear of chocolate on the side of his mouth.

There was a scraping of chairs as some of the bridal party stood. "What's going on?" Kelly asked, looking curious.

"The killer's in the basement," a man at a table near the sergeant's shouted.

"We're coming too," Kaitlyn said, glancing shyly at Gaurav.

With Eve leading the way, we all ran down the stairs to the basement. I hoped that Gerry had found the trousers and put them somewhere we could easily find them. That is, if the trousers were actually there. What if I'd pulled everyone into this laundry fiasco and nothing turned up? I'd look like I'd lost my marbles. I brushed away the idea. Balanced against catching a murderer, looking foolish seemed worth the gamble.

Eve panted as she thumbed through her huge set of keys. "Gotcha," she said, putting the right key into the lock. I held my breath as she opened the door.

A plump woman had an ironing board set up on one side of the large cellar room. A dryer was running, and the large washer had its door open, like a hungry mouth waiting to be fed. She had a bag of laundry in her hand and was reading the label.

"That's Gwendolyn," Eve said. "She's in charge of our overnight service."

Oh no! If those trousers had been laundered already, they wouldn't be able to provide the evidence I needed.

Gerry was trying to block Gwendolyn, and as I watched, he managed to make her drop the bag. "Pops, the trousers are in that bag, but I can't lift them out without giving this poor lady a heart attack."

"Stop her!" I yelled.

Gwendolyn turned round abruptly. She looked stunned, as well she might. She'd probably never had an out-of-breath group of people rush into the laundry room before.

"Sorry," I said. "But what's in that bag is really important."

She lifted the sack. "In here? Only a bunch of smelly clothes in here. You want to wait until I've washed em, love."

And maybe some grass-stained ones, too.

"Could I take a quick peek?"

Gwendolyn shot Eve a look that read, *Is this chick for real?* Eve nodded, and Gwendolyn shrugged. "Knock yourself out, darling."

I took a deep breath, preparing myself to delve into a bag of nasties, but Gerry said, "Don't worry. They're right on top."

I spotted the cream silk immediately. I pinched the fabric between my thumb and middle finger and pulled out the trousers. I carefully unrolled them. Just as I'd thought. The bottom was flecked with mud and covered in bits of grass.

Suddenly a voice said, "What are they doing with your trousers, Jessica?"

In unison, the group turned. It was Joe. He was extremely pale. And by his side was Jessica, who was even whiter than her husband. She looked terrified. They must have followed us down here.

"I haven't a clue," she said in a small voice. "They're just dirty trousers."

I walked over to Sgt. Lane and lifted the cuff of the cream satin. "See how it's covered in grass?" I said. "Well, I had the same problem." I lifted my sneakers and pointed at the green stains. "It happened while I was at the Orangery, picking flowers to decorate the wedding cake." I looked hard at Jessica. "The wedding cake you begged me to bake as a special surprise for your best friend."

She lowered her eyes.

"Edward, the gardener, mowed around the wedding venue that morning, but he only raked where the guests would be. He didn't have time to finish, so the area near the stream was never raked. So anyone who has bits of grass on the bottom of their trousers had to have been near the stream."

"Which is where we found the murder weapon," Sgt. Lane said.

I nodded. "The cupid statue."

Everyone gasped, including Gwendolyn.

"So, I walked down to the stream," Jessica said. "I wanted a bit of air. That doesn't prove anything."

I stepped forward. "But you were wearing these trousers. You didn't have them on when you were decorating the venue. You changed for dinner."

"I took a walk after dinner," she said, sounding lame.

A sudden freeze went over the crowd and I saw Lauren come forward. She was staring at Jessica as though she'd never seen her before.

Jessica saw her and said, sounding desperate, "You know what a perfectionist I am, Lauren. Had to do a final check."

"And walk all the way to the edge of the stream?" I countered.

Florence edged past me and looked at the cardboard ticket that had to be filled out to go along with the laundry. She shook her head and looked at Jessica. "Only a murderer would put pure, cream-colored silk into a regular laundry machine." She waved the card around. "And see here? She's specified it's to be washed in hot water. It would ruin the trousers."

"But it would remove grass stains," I said. "And, hopefully, whatever other evidence was on the clothes she wore when she killed Ryan Blandford."

"No," Lauren said, backing away.

Sgt. Lane turned to face Joe. "Perhaps you'd care to rethink what you told me earlier."

Joe looked horrified. As well he might. He nodded. "I lied. I'm sorry. I didn't arrive until after one a.m. Jessica said it would look better for me if she told you guys she'd been with me all night. I agreed, thinking she was giving me an alibi. I never clued in that I was giving her one. She'd convinced me that if it came out that I knew she and Ryan had been having an affair, it would have made me the prime suspect."

So Joe did know. Wow, Ryan and Jessica hadn't exactly been careful while they sneaked around. Worst adulterers ever.

"No," Lauren moaned.

Joe stared at his wife. "I don't understand. Why would you kill him? You told me you loved him."

Jessica covered her face with her hands. "He ended it. Said he only wanted to be with her. How could I bear it? Seeing them together all the time when he should have been with me? Years ago, he told me he wasn't the marrying kind, so I went ahead and married you, Joe. He came to our room to tell me it was over. I begged him to reconsider, and he said he should have stopped it as soon as he began dating Lauren.

"He said he was going out to get some air, and I followed

177

him. He walked up to the Orangery, and I could see he was thinking of the wonderful life he had planned. Without me! I was so angry. I tackled him, and we argued. He said I was a terrible wife and a terrible friend. I just saw red. I wasn't even thinking. I grabbed the cupid statue that was supposed to bring lovers together and whacked him over the head. I regretted it instantly, but it was too late. He was dead."

Sgt. Lane walked up to Jessica. "Let's go down to the station," he said, "and you can make your statement."

"Joe!" But Joe wouldn't return her gaze. He hung his head.

"Lauren! I never meant for this to happen. You never would have known."

"Get away from me," the bride shouted. "I trusted you. You were my best friend. And you killed the man I loved." She turned and fled.

The group watched in silence as Sgt. Lane handcuffed Jessica and read her her rights. Even though I'd been certain the culprit was Jessica, part of me was still shocked. I recalled our phone conversation last week. She'd been so enthusiastic about giving her best friend a dream wedding, helping to organize every little detail. The way she'd fussed over the decorations, retying the lilac bows, arranging for more oranges on the trees. Now I could see that the guilt had been motivating it all. How could she do that to her best friend? And keep it secret right until their wedding day? I couldn't imagine doing that to Gina––ever. No man should come between friends; the bond was too precious.

The sergeant led the murderer away.

Florence finally broke the silence in the laundry room. "And let that be a lesson to all of us. If you've got murder on your mind, wear the proper clothing."

Not exactly the message we all needed to hear, but she had helped crack the case.

"To think Jessica would have got away with murder if it hadn't been for you spotting those grass stains, Poppy," Hamish said. "And you, Florence, getting her to confess. You've both done us proud today."

"And Gaurav even managed to get a date out of it," Florence added.

Poor Gaurav looked mortified. "That wasn't my only intention."

"We know," said Priscilla gently. "Added bonus."

"I don't think I'll be using the next-day laundry service again in a hurry," Florence said, shivering. "It's put me off."

We headed back up to the pub, our pace much more leisurely now that a murderer was no longer on the loose. I should have been exhausted, but the adrenaline was still coursing through my veins. The events of the last fifteen minutes had felt like a lifetime. I think my heartbeat may have even stopped once or twice. I felt switched on, buzzing from the magnitude of what had just happened. Maybe a small nightcap would sort me out. Hamish suggested a dram of whiskey which sounded about right. I needed a good night's sleep before tomorrow's showstopper.

Eve wiped her brow. "That was enough excitement to last a lifetime. I'm actually relieved to go back to the kitchen to finish service. Having to serve up twelve apple crumbles suddenly feels like child's play compared to what my nerves have just been through." She kissed me on the cheek and whispered into my ear, "Well done, little sister." The words made me glow. *Little sister.*

"Shall we have a toast?" Florence said to the group.

"Oh no, you don't, you naughty bakers."

It was Elspeth who seemed to have appeared out of nowhere. "You all need an early night to be ready to make your showstopper first thing."

There was a collective groan.

"No complaining. Time for bed!" she admonished. She might well have said: And remember to get in the carriage before it turns back into a pumpkin.

Maybe Elspeth was *everyone's* fairy godmother.

CHAPTER 15

The morning of the showstopper, I awoke from a deep sleep. I'd been dreaming—not the usual nightmares about burning caramel. Or murderers. Instead, a shadowy figure was singing me a song. It was lilting and gentle, and she had a beautiful voice. Fragments of the melody were still in my head. It sounded familiar and comforting. I was sure I'd heard that song somewhere before, but in the half-world between sleep and waking, I'd lost the memory of where.

I rolled out of bed, for once feeling refreshed and ready for the challenge ahead. I was going to create a fabulous showstopper and secure my place in the next round. It was going to be Positive Poppy from now on. Bye-bye negative energy.

A quick shower, and then I pulled on yesterday's outfit, dusting off a speck of flour still clinging to the fabric. I paused while lacing up my white sneakers, meditating for a moment on the green stain that had led me to the truth about Ryan's murder. It really went to show that the devil was in the details. And I was going to have to be as equally meticulous baking today. Full steam ahead.

The theme for this week's showstopper was to render famous European monuments in cake form. Call me a masochist, but I'd been looking forward to this challenge all week. It was just so fun! I'd had a great idea for my monument: Saint Basil's Cathedral in Moscow's Red Square. Gina had argued that Russia was really in Asia and had me so freaked that I called the show producers and checked. They decreed that Moscow was considered to be in the European part of Russia. Phew.

Although I'd never been, I'd seen photographs of the famous building in a travel magazine and was instantly taken with its unusual shape, red and white brick, and use of bold colors. It was full of grandeur—perfect for a showstopper showdown. The construction was going to be the hardest part: the base, five towers, and turrets I'd make from sponge, the domes from baby meringues. But choosing the flavor had been easy: soft red velvet sponge inside and red and white fondant icing to create the bold patterns on the outside of the cathedral. The finished cake should look flamboyant and fun. At least that was the plan.

I'd done my research and, like Jonathon, had prepared some talking points about this monument's rich history. I was intrigued to see what the other bakers had chosen...not to mention worried that someone else had picked the same building.

Downstairs, everyone apart from Florence (go figure) was already eating breakfast. I smiled at the group. We'd really come together last night, and this morning felt a little bit like waking up in a beloved holiday home and coming downstairs to find your extended family tucking into eggs and bacon.

After my healthy(ish) salad last night, I needed a serious plate of food-energy, so I loaded up on the whole-grain toast, scrambled eggs, fried tomatoes and mushrooms. A cup of strong black coffee and I'd be set.

I took a seat next to Gaurav, and we discussed the details of Jessica's arrest. But Hamish put a stop to our chatter. "One thing I've learned from years on the force is that you've got to leave work at work," he said. "You can't bring it home with you, otherwise it eats you—and today, our job is to bake things the judges want to eat. Eyes on the prize."

Hamish was right, of course. I'd learned my lesson last week after my disastrous performance in the tent. No more shop talk.

To my surprise, Florence actually made it down to breakfast in time to eat with everyone else. She looked perfect, although she admitted that receiving her fresh laundry this morning hadn't been the dreamy scenario she'd previously imagined.

Hamish stopped her, reiterating his point. "It's show-stopper day, and we need to live and breathe cake."

Florence laughed and raised her glass of freshly squeezed orange juice. "To cake," she said.

"To cake."

For the first time since the show began, all of the contestants arrived for filming together. I entered the tent and felt the frantic energy of the crew as they rushed around, putting the last-minute touches to ready the set for another long day's shoot. The director, Fiona, was pacing, and Donald Friesen, the series producer, was back on set and stressed as usual.

That man was going to have a heart attack before he turned fifty if he wasn't careful.

Gina was waiting by her makeup station. And by the look on her face, she'd heard all about Jessica's arrest.

I held up my hands. "I know what you're going to say."

Gina wagged a finger at me. "Oh, you do, do you?"

"Yes. You're going to tell me that I need to be careful and stay away from danger. That I'm your best friend in the whole world and you need me, so please no more sleuthing on the side."

Gina burst out laughing. "Pretty much word for word what I wanted to say. Well done. Now heed my excellent advice, will you?"

"I promise to be careful. But I can't ignore my instincts, either. If I have a hunch, I have to follow it."

Without thinking, I touched the amethyst necklace. So far, I'd managed to escape danger, despite spending some of my free time with murderers. How much did I owe my safety to its protection? Was it powerful enough to keep me away from all harm? Did it work in tandem with the protection spell Elspeth gave me? And where did my own abilities fit in this equation?

Gina frowned. "I think I understand, but remember I consider it my job to look out for you. Particularly how pale you look today. But don't worry, Doctor Bronzer is going to magic that away."

I grinned. "I appreciate it."

I sat in the chair. "Gina, do I look dowdy to you?"

"Dowdy?" She wrinkled her nose. "Of course not. What's all this about?"

I told her what Florence had said about me not being able to pull off glamor.

She leaned closer. "Let me tell you something, Poppy. Florence might look like a film star, but she's not as popular as you."

I didn't believe it, but Gina was my best friend, and it was her job to cheer me up. "I have eyes, Gina. Men worship her, and women long to look like her."

"I listen to the people who come and watch the taping. You're a lot more popular. Do you know why?"

I shook my head. I didn't believe her, anyway.

"Because you're likable. You're the kind of person a man could imagine being with and women want to be friends with. Florence intimidates both sexes. I'd watch out for her. She's starting to show her teeth because you're doing so well in the competition. She's a classic frenemy."

"No. Stop. I don't want to think that. She's always been so friendly." Then I thought about Jessica and Lauren being best friends. Look how that had turned out.

"Shall I do her hair in such a way that it falls out halfway through the first hour? Or put on the special mascara that melts in the heat?"

"No." But I giggled all the same. It was good having Gina on set. I told her all about last night while Gina did her magic. As for my own magic, all I had to do was bake and decorate the replica of a world-famous monument.

Catching murderers seemed easier.

AT MY WORKSTATION, I began setting up, getting my ingredients and equipment ready and running through each stage of my bake in my mind. I was focused and ready.

Robbie, the sound guy, came over to test my mic. He leaned in. "I'm not supposed to say anything to the contestants about the show, but I want you to know that I'm rooting for you, Poppy."

I blushed. How nice. Maybe Gina hadn't completely been blowing smoke. Okay, maybe silk trousers weren't in my future, but being likable was good.

Fiona finally called action, and the four hosts entered the tent together. It fell to Jonathon to introduce the showstopper challenge.

"Each of you must interpret a famous European landmark. Whether it be biscuit or sponge, meringue or cheesecake, we want innovation, ingenuity, and great-tasting monuments. We want to be wowed."

Arty stepped forward. "And that's what I call a *monumental* challenge." Arty said, pausing for the laughter and groans at another terrible pun. "Wowing these two judges won't be easy," he added—as if we needed reminding. "You should try to imagine that your creations are going to be the centerpiece of a celebrity party. Or maybe even the wedding cake for when Jilly decides to make an honest man of me."

Everyone gasped. Was this another joke? Or did Arty just admit to their relationship? On screen, no less.

Jilly looked stunned. After a beat of silence, she laughed nervously. "Arty, your jokes are getting worse every week. Bakers, your time starts...now."

Florence and I said our usual good lucks, and then it was straight on to mixing the red velvet batter. I'd been making this recipe with my mom since I was knee-high, and to my mind, it had a superior buttery, vanilla, and cocoa flavor, as well as a delicious tang from buttermilk. To get a smooth, velvet crumb, I whipped the egg whites, which was worth the extra time.

Elspeth and Jilly approached my workstation, and I steeled myself to talk through my showstopper. But the lighting guy called out that he needed to adjust the brightness, so I continued mixing while Elspeth and Jilly waited, watching me crack eggs. I felt suddenly shy and unsure of myself. But when Elspeth touched my arm for a moment, all calm was restored. "That smells heavenly," she said, peering into my cake mix.

I smiled. *You've got this, Pops.*

When we got the go-ahead from Fiona, the director, to start rolling, Jilly spoke first. "Poppy, you've definitely got a challenge on your hands today. Can you tell us more about why you chose St. Basil's Cathedral in Moscow's Red Square?"

Like Jonathon, I'd prepared my lines about this piece of history. "Well, I've not been lucky enough to visit Russia, but I have always been fascinated by architecture. Maybe it's my graphic design background. I love striking shapes, and a photograph of the cathedral in a magazine drew my eye immediately. It's so different from the style of building I grew up around—both here and in the States. St. Basil's Cathedral in particular is very sculptural, with high towers topped with onion-shaped domes—but don't worry, no onions in this recipe."

Jilly laughed. "You stole the joke right out of my mouth."

"The cathedral resides in Moscow's famous Red Square. It

was built in 1591 and has stood through centuries of turbulent history. It's a survivor. And I hope my cake version is, too. No crumbling, please.

"I had a lot of fun making the sketches for this showstopper." I'd found dozens of images online and drawn it from all angles so that I could make a 3D sketch, which, of course, had been filmed for the introduction when they put the show together.

Elspeth smiled. "And you're doing a red velvet mix?"

"Yes. I thought since I couldn't replicate the whole square, I could play on the red element using a red velvet recipe I've been making for years."

They wished me luck and moved on to Florence. Her chosen monument was the Coliseum, and she was busy mixing up a chocolate sponge for the center. I listened in to her prepared monologue. Oh, she was good.

"I'm using Vanini chocolate," she was saying in her silky voice. "It's the best you can find in Italy. It has a smooth, mellow flavor, which is great for this twice-baked recipe. It's going to have two distinct textures. A crunchy base and an oozing center. I'll purposely overbake the bottom layer and underbake the top layer."

Jonathon joined their workstation and listened carefully.

"Sounds risky," Elspeth said.

"It is, but I hope it'll pay off," Florence replied.

"At least you're not in danger of a soggy bottom," Jilly added. "No one wants one of those."

"Agreed." Florence laughed. "And then I'll cover the cake in a light layer of butterscotch buttercream to get the color of ancient stone."

"I wonder if the whole thing might end up being too rich," Jonathon said.

At that, Florence whipped her head up. She seemed momentarily fazed by Jonathon's reservations but then pulled herself together again.

"It's a balancing act between richness and a warm, mellow flavor," Florence said, her hands making abstractions in the air. "I can only hope to impress."

Jonathon nodded solemnly.

Florence looked glum. "Don't worry," I whispered when the judges moved on. "Jonathon can be abrupt like that, but I think he's a pussycat really."

Florence raised an eyebrow. "You reckon? He terrifies me."

I recalled Jonathon reciting his lines again, the way he softly joined in the chant during the magic circle for Susan Bentley. If only I could share these snapshots of our judge with Florence, but of course I couldn't.

"Don't worry. It sounds up to your usual fabulous standards."

Florence smiled. Her pearly-white teeth gleamed.

My cake batter ready, I poured it into three square tins and a loaf tin, which I'd use to form the towers. I slid the lot into the oven, super aware of the camera following me, and wished it well in my mind. *Go forth and rise, little cakes.*

Now I had to turn my attention to the towers' meringue domes. I had my food coloring at the ready: green, yellow, red, blue, white and orange. I'd swirl a few drops of each into separate meringue mixes. This really was a lot of work, and the clock was ticking.

As I whipped my egg whites and sugar, I listened to

Priscilla explain her showstopper to Elspeth. Priscilla was clearly out to impress, attempting to construct a biscuit Eiffel Tower. But I did wonder if she'd bitten off more than she could chew. I groaned at my own accidental pun. I was getting as bad as Arty.

Jonathon was saying, "Connecting all the different parts is going to be tricky. You'll need a really sturdy base to support that framework."

And from the looks of it, she was going to have trouble keeping it all together.

"Yes," she said, sounding nervous. "I'm using vanilla and almond biscuits, which I'll decorate with gold leaf to make it look like the Eiffel Tower when it's lit up with twinkling lights at nighttime."

Then Jilly announced that we had two hours left, and I had no time to eavesdrop. There was a lot of work to do in two hours before we'd have to present to the judges.

I felt myself get into the groove of baking, losing myself in the familiar rhythm of each stage of this whopper. The cream cheese frosting to sandwich the sponges together, the vanilla fondant icing to smooth over the outside. This last bit I was especially worried about: The fondant would need to be rolled extra thin so as not to put too much pressure on my cream cheese frosting inside the cake. And then I'd have to get clean lines for the bold patterns on the towers. So much to think about, so little time.

But as usual, the hours flew by. Before I knew it, I was putting the final touches to the outside of my cathedral when Jonathon called out that our time was up.

I stood back from my workstation, a little amazed at what I'd managed to produce. The cathedral was beautiful, bold and eye-catching, and I'd managed to get exactly the right shape for the meringue turrets. I was proud of my hard work.

Jonathon and Elspeth approached the judging table, bringing with them a bundle of what looked to be flashcards. Were they planning a spot-test on sponge or something? My stomach went cold, and I had visions of sweating in the back of high school math class. Surely they wouldn't be so cruel? Together, they moved around the table and set a card by each cake. Oh! They were blown-up photographs of the real monuments. What a neat touch.

"This is a very impressive array of cakes," Elspeth said. "Just looking at your showstoppers makes me feel like I've been on a cruise around the world."

"Ideas for your next holiday, perhaps?" Arty suggested.

"Despite my grand age, Arty, I don't think I'm much of a cruise person. A hike in the Alps is more my style."

"Point taken," Arty said sheepishly.

"But more to the point, let's see what these cakes taste like," said Jonathon, brandishing knife and fork.

Up first was Hamish. He'd made a rose- and pistachio-flavored Acropolis. The grand row of pillars looked magnificent and must have been hard to get right. He'd replicated the color of ancient stone perfectly with an almond fondant icing.

"Looks very realistic," Elspeth said.

"But the proof is in the pudding," Jonathon replied, cutting into the Acropolis so a column fell over.

But Elspeth and Jonathon got busy tasting. From the look on Jonathon's face, he was about to say something devastating.

"I'm afraid it's very dry, Hamish," Jonathon said.

And there it was.

Elspeth nodded. "Lovely flavor pairings, but I'm afraid I have to agree with Jonathon that it's on the dry side."

Hamish looked downcast.

The judges swiftly moved on to Maggie's rendition of Gaudí's Sagrada Família, which I'd heard Maggie tell the judges was a Roman Catholic minor basilica in Barcelona, Spain. She'd outdone herself. The cake was huge, with dramatic high spires in the elongated Gaudí style. Elspeth and Jonathon were impressed, too.

"I honestly don't know how you managed to get the spires that thin and still hold the structure," Jonathon said admiringly. And, of course, they loved the cake. It was almond and orange, two celebrated Spanish ingredients. Maggie beamed under their praise.

Then it was Priscilla's turn. Poor Priscilla. Jonathon looked at the monument. "Looks more like the Leaning Tower of Pisa than the Eiffel Tower." There was a definite tilt to the structure, which threatened to collapse at any moment.

"It was a brave attempt, though," Elspeth said. "I particularly like the gold leaf effect. Now, let's see how it tastes."

As they tried to break off a piece of biscuit, the whole thing came toppling down. It was like a small explosion. Cookies jumped, and gold leaf sprayed into the air. I saw the glee on the cameraman's face as he moved closer. It would make a great TV moment.

Priscilla put her head in her hands for the second time this weekend.

The two judges sampled the biscuits and pronounced them flavorful but I don't think Priscilla even heard the compliment.

Gaurav's Arc de Triomphe was next. It was a sponge cake with a berry and cream filling, covered in fondant icing. Both judges declared the structure a triumph and the cake itself fruity, mouth-watering and moist. Praise indeed.

Daniel's Blue Mosque was absolutely huge.

"You could see that cake from space," Jilly commented.

Both judges agreed that it had a lovely flavor, but its huge size and the stack of blueberries decorating the top weighed down the Genoese sponge, which should have been light and airy.

Amara had made the actual Leaning Tower of Pisa, as opposed to Priscilla's accidental one. She received similar feedback to Daniel, but Elspeth did say she really enjoyed the very Italian combination of apricot and amaretto that married perfectly with Amara's frangipane base.

Finally it was time for my beautiful cathedral to meet its end in the taste test.

"This is very good-looking, Poppy," Jonathon said. "You've gone the extra mile, and it shows. That's a fine, smooth finish on the fondant. But let's see if it's squashed your cream cheese frosting inside."

I held my breath as they sliced it open. If the weight of the fondant had damaged the texture of the inside, then it was curtains for me.

But to my relief, the sponge was unharmed.

Elspeth took a mouthful. "It's sweet. It's creamy. It's moist. Delicious. A wonderful creation."

I glowed. I'd baked my little heart out, but was it enough to keep me in the competition?

Luckily, the agony of waiting to hear our fate wasn't

prolonged. After a few moments conferring, Elspeth and Jonathon announced they'd made a decision.

Poor Priscilla was once again in last place. I lost the plot a bit waiting for my name, and then we'd arrived at third place, and they still hadn't called my name.

Jonathon spoke first. "In third place, Gaurav."

"It was a tough call between our runner-up and winner," Elspeth went on. "But in second place is Florence."

Another top three for Florence. She'd be pleased. But wait, I still hadn't heard my name. Had I missed it?

"And this week's winner is…"

In the silence, I could almost hear the name "Maggie" echo in the tent.

Jonathon cleared his throat. "Poppy!"

"What?" I said, totally confused. "I won?"

I was stunned. But before I could process the news properly, it was time for the worst part of each episode.

Arty's voice was grave. "As you know, we have to ask someone to leave the tent today, and that someone is going to be Priscilla."

Even though it was disappointing, it wasn't much of a surprise. She nodded.

And the best baker of this week's episode?

Once more I heard my name announced and nearly fell off my stool.

Then, suddenly, filming was done for another week. We mingled, hugging and chatting, with the cameras still rolling.

Elspeth turned to Priscilla and took both her hands. "You've been a true star, and it's been a pleasure to have you on the show."

"The pleasure's been all mine," Priscilla said, sniffing a

little but smiling bravely. "It's been such an exciting experience. Thank you."

I got lots of congratulations and was nearly floating on air. What a weekend!

We crowded round Priscilla, trying to show how much we loved her by squeezing the life out of her. She giggled and said, "Get off. You're ruining my hair!"

CHAPTER 16

On our way back to the pub, everyone was in high spirits. Even Priscilla.

"To tell you the truth, Poppy," she said, walking beside me, "I was getting tired of the pressure. It was wearing me down. I'm used to standing on my feet all day cutting hair and dealing with high-maintenance clients, but this was something else. I'm exhausted."

"I know what you mean. At the start of every weekend I feel like I'm going into battle. And then when it's over, I have to start prepping for the next one."

"My friends and family will be glad to have me back for Saturday brunches and Sunday pub lunches, too," she said.

"Isn't that the dream," I said, smiling.

"And Harry said he wants to keep in touch. I'm glad I'll have more time. He needs a friend."

"He does." And I really hoped Priscilla and he would enjoy spending time together. Who knew what might come out of this tragedy?

As for me, I was delighted to be back in the game. I loved

being in Broomewode. I loved the thrill of the bake. And I loved the people I'd met along the way.

I looked around at the immaculate lawns surrounding the old house, happy in the knowledge I'd be back again next week. So my cunning plan to work alongside the Broomewode Hall staff hadn't come to much, but with the return of Katie Donegal, I was a little wiser. Valerie had definitely become pregnant while she was working here, and then she'd disappeared without a trace. My dad could still live around here or maybe he was in London. I was getting closer to answers.

I turned back and saw Edward, the gardener, waving at me to come over. I told Priscilla I'd meet her and the rest of the bakers in the pub and jogged to Edward.

He told me that he'd just finished his shift and was about to walk back into town. It had been a long weekend, and he was bone tired. "I'm not cut out for all the drama that's been happening in Broomewode Village."

I nodded in sympathy. I knew the feeling.

"I saw Lauren earlier. We went for a walk. But I heard your weekend was intense, too," he said. "How did you know the killer was Jessica?"

"Actually, you played a part in solving that mystery."

Edward looked baffled.

"It was her grass stains."

He looked even more bemused. I was getting really good at eliciting this kind of response from people.

"After you cut the grass, you raked the area where the wedding guests would be. But not around the stream. Sly, Susan's dog, ran in after his ball and came out covered in bits of grass. They stuck to my sneakers, too. I guessed that if

Jessica had thrown the murder weapon into the stream, she'd have the same bits of mown grass on her trousers. And she did."

Edward didn't look thrilled with my detective work as much as crestfallen. "You're telling me it was my sloppy job that cracked the case? I didn't think I needed to rake down there, too. Only so many hours in the day and all."

"Don't be so hard on yourself. You stopped someone getting away with murder."

Edward whistled through his teeth. "Well then, I vow to rake less often in the name of justice. But, more importantly, are you through to the next round?"

My huge grin must have given it away because Edward started laughing.

"Officially, I'm not supposed to say, but I won the show-stopper challenge and was crowned best baker this week."

He congratulated me with a hearty thwack on the back. "I'm going to get out of these overalls and then I'll see you in the pub."

I turned in the direction of the inn, ready to celebrate with a glass of something fizzy, but something drew me toward the ornamental lake. It was a strange feeling. The same one I'd had when I felt drawn to the stream. Was this my fate as a water witch? To be pulled toward any body of water I might pass? That seemed pretty inconvenient. But since my instincts had served me well over the last few days, I followed them and went to the water's edge.

The lake was lovely in the afternoon sun. The swans were serene and elegant as they floated past water lilies and cattails. A few green-headed mallards dove for food, their fluffy behinds sticking out of the water. I stayed there for a moment, watching the water's surface, remembering the first vision I'd ever had. The blurry silhouette of a woman running, the bump of her pregnancy. Now I knew it was my mother, and I closed my eyes, hoping for another image to appear on the rippling surface. I still had so many unanswered questions. Why had Valerie fled Broomewode Hall? Why had Katie Donegal been so reluctant to tell what she knew? Where was Valerie? And where was my father? Did he still live nearby? Did he even know that I existed? I thought back to the magic circle, when a ghostly figure had appeared to me. Could it be that the man in my vision from the magic circle was actually my dad?

I squeezed my eyes tighter and tried to conjure up an image of my mother. I desperately wanted to see her face. Could visions be brought on with the same concentration as my telekinesis? There was only one way to find out. I took every ounce of energy I had left in my body and focused on what I knew about my mother. In my mind's eye, I saw the photograph Eileen had given me of Valerie laughing in a summer dress; the shawl draped across the shoulders of the countess; the voice that had spoken to me from the bath, warning me that I was in danger. And that's when I heard it again: soft, gentle humming, a familiar melody. The song from my dream. My whole body began to tingle. My heart thumped in my chest. Suddenly my whole body went cold. I opened my eyes slowly, too afraid of seeing nothing, of being disappointed. But there she was. Valerie. I took in a deep breath. She was in profile, staring at something I couldn't see. She looked older than the photograph I had, tired around the eyes. But happy. She stopped humming and began to sing:

I know where I'm going
And I know who's going with me
I know who I love
And the dear knows who I'll marry.

I have stockings of silk
And shoes of bright green leather
Combs to buckle my hair
And a ring for every finger.

Some say he's poor
But I say he's bonnie
The fairest of them all
My handsome winsome Johnny.

Feather beds are soft
And painted rooms are bonny
But I would leave them all
To go with my love, my Johnny.

I know where I'm going
And I know who's going with me
I know who I love
But the dear knows who I'll marry.

I listened in wonder. I knew the words. Every line. The lyrics were buried inside me somewhere, long forgotten. But now it was coming back. My heart was in my throat.

"Mom?" I said. "Can you hear me?"

She turned her face toward me. The reflection rippled.

"Poppy, you were born out of love. You must stop searching for answers."

I opened my mouth to answer, but she disappeared. The electricity coursing through my body dulled, and I felt warm again.

"Come back!" I yelled at the now-smooth water. "There's so much I need to know. Why should I stop asking questions?" A duck flapped its wings and suddenly flew away. Then there was silence.

I sat for a moment by the lake's edge, devastated. Why appear only to vanish again seconds later? Had I angered her somehow? All I wanted was the truth. Was that a lullaby she was singing? I knew the words as if I'd written the song myself. I couldn't do what she asked. I needed to know where I came from.

I stood, dusting down my dress. I wasn't going to give up. "I'm sorry, Mom," I whispered. "It's just too important to let go."

I walked back to the inn, my earlier elation dampened, but I was still heartened by the song. It was another clue to the mystery around my birth. I was certain now that I'd heard that song sung to me as a baby.

A hawk swooped past me as I walked. It looked like the same one I'd seen yesterday. It was a beautiful bird and as I watched it did a circle around me and then flew back toward Broomewode Hall.

IN THE PUB, I heard the other bakers before I saw them. Loud, raucous laughter filled the room, and there was the tell-tale pop of a Prosecco bottle opening. I straightened up, rearranged my hair and decided to put my best face forward. I'd arrived this weekend worried I'd be sent home, and instead I was best baker.

I was about to take a seat when I saw that some of the wedding party were leaving. Kaitlyn went up to Gaurav, and they hugged goodbye. Naturally, I strained to hear what they were saying, but they kept their voices low. And then, with a final wave, she left.

Gaurav looked sheepish and sat down again. I took the seat next to him, and Florence promptly filled an empty glass with bubbles.

"To another fabulous week of baking," she said.

"And to good friends," I added.

We clinked glasses. There was a loud "ahem," and the whole group turned to see Joe loitering by Florence. He looked embarrassed. "Can I speak to you?"

"Of course." She excused herself and walked outside with him.

I caught Hamish's eye and raised a brow.

We went back to talking about the cakes we'd made, the fears we'd had, all the usual post-filming chat until Florence returned. In her hands was a business card.

"He gave you his business card?" Daniel asked.

She flipped it over. "With his home and mobile numbers on the back." She folded the card in half and put it inside an empty Walkers Crisps packet. "Too much baggage," she said.

I spotted Lauren saying goodbye to Eve. I couldn't catch what they were saying, but Eve hugged her tight. Edward walked in, wearing jeans now, and watched her go.

"And her baggage is even heavier," Florence said, her eyes on Edward as he lingered at the bar.

"I'd say he's got a strong back," Hamish said quietly.

"And that's what we'll all need," Daniel said, looking grim. "Any one of us remaining contestants is good enough to win. So, from now on, the challenges will only get more difficult."

"How do we win, then?" Florence asked.

"Stay focused."

"And that goes double for you, Poppy," Gerry said, sitting in Daniel's lap. "No more side trips down murder lane."

I wanted to argue that I didn't go looking for trouble, but I couldn't.

Gerry chuckled. "The thing I like best about being a ghost is I always get the last word."

A Note from Nancy

Dear Reader,

Thank you for reading The Great Witches Baking Show series. I am so grateful for all the enthusiasm this series has received. I hope you'll consider leaving a review and please tell your friends who like cozy mysteries and culinary adventures.

Review on Amazon, Goodreads or BookBub.

Your support is appreciated. Turn the page for a sneak peek of Blood, Sweat and Tiers, the next book in the series, and Poppy's recipe for Poppy's Lemon and Lavender Bundt Cake.

Join my newsletter at nancywarren.net to hear about my new releases and special offers.

I hope to see you in my private Facebook Group. It's a lot of fun. www.facebook.com/groups/NancyWarrenKnitwits

Until next time,
Happy Reading,

Nancy

Chapter 1

"Why is that man coming toward us with a rifle?" Florence asked, moving so she stood behind Hamish's broad back. We all looked up from our workstations in the competition tent at Broomewode, in Somerset. It was Friday afternoon and we were preparing for this weekend's baking competition.

As well as a few keen baking contestants, the tent contained technicians setting up lights checking sound and making sure we'd be ready to roll early tomorrow morning.

I recognized the man with the gun, even if Florence didn't. "That's the Earl of Frome," I told her. "Don't worry. He won't shoot us. He needs the money from the Great British Baking Contest to run the estate."

Hamish added, "And that's not a rifle. It's a shotgun meant for hunting game not killing people. It's broken which means he can't shoot it." Hamish was a Scottish police officer, but he raised Shetland ponies and knew all about farming. By broken, I assumed he meant the way the barrel was bent away from the stock of the gun so it looked like a triangle. The earl had another man following behind also carrying a shotgun. I'd lived in the English countryside long enough to recognize that they wore hunting tweeds. Wool caps, tweed jackets with matching vests over jodhpurs tucked into leather boots. Under the vest and jacket they wore checked shirts with ties.

The earl came into the tent. It was the first time I'd ever seen him do so. "Afternoon," he said in his posh voice. "How are you all getting on?"

"Fine," Hamish said and Florence and I nodded.

"Good, good."

Fiona, the director, came in then and glanced at the gun with horror. "Are you going shooting, Sir?"

"Not to worry. Won't make a noise while you're filming. Thought I'd pop in and give you all my best." He spied the fresh raspberries on Florence's workstation. "What lovely, fresh berries. Local, I imagine."

Florence was never one to pass up an opportunity. "Yes, your Lordship. Please, help yourself." He popped a red berry into his mouth and made noises indicative of pleasure. Florence said, "It's cake week, you see, your Lordship. The judges want us to use some of the local, fresh fruits."

"Marvelous. Marvelous." Then he looked as though he'd run out of conversation. "Well, carry on. I look forward to seeing your cakes."

And then he was gone. When he was out of earshot Hamish turned to Florence with a grin. "Your Lordship?"

"I looked up how one should address an Earl for just such an occasion," she said with dignity.

We watched as Lord Frome and the man who was

presumably his gamekeeper headed off down a path. The earl stumbled over a root and Hamish said, "Let's hope he doesn't shoot his own foot off."

Order your copy today! *Blood, Sweat and Tiers* is Book 5 in the Great Witches Baking Show series.

POPPY'S LEMON AND LAVENDER BUNDT CAKE

Ingredients:

Lavender and Lemon Sponge:

- ½ cup unsalted butter at room temperature
- 1 cup sugar
- 1½ cups flour
- 2 large eggs
- ½ cup buttermilk
- ¼ teaspoon salt
- ¼ teaspoon baking soda
- 1¼ teaspoon dried lavender
- zest of 1 lemon
- 1 teaspoon of vanilla extract
- 2 tablespoons of fresh lemon juice
- 1¼ teaspoon of dried lavender buds

The Glaze

- 1 cup of powdered sugar
- 2 teaspoons buttermilk
- 1 tablespoon fresh lemon juice

Method:

1. First up, you're going to need to get that oven preheated. 325 degrees Fahrenheit should do it.
2. Butter your Bundt tin and then set aside.
3. Now on to the good stuff. Combine your sugar and lemon zest in a mixing bowl, mashing the two together with the back of a spoon until the sugar becomes wet and fragrant.
4. Now it's time to add that room-temperature butter and cream it with the lemony sugar until you have a fluffy mix. This should take about three minutes if you're using a good ol' electric mixer like me.
5. Once you're happy with the consistency, add the eggs one at a time, mixing thoroughly after each addition.
6. Now it's time to get those yummy liquids involved. Combine your buttermilk, vanilla extract, and lemon juice in a measuring cup.
7. In a separate bowl, sift your flour, baking soda and salt.
8. Now for the uplifting part of your bake. Take the lavender buds and crush them with the tips of your fingers in the palm of your hand—breathe their scent deeply for the ultimate burst of nature's relaxant—and then add the crushed buds to your flour mixture.

9. Put your mixer on a low setting, and then alternately add the flour mixture and the buttermilk mixture, beginning and ending with the flour mixture, in 3 additions.

10. Pour batter into prepared 6-cup Bundt pan, smoothing the top with the back of a spatula.

11. Bake for 40-50 minutes. Check for doneness with a toothpick. It'll be ready when your toothpick comes out clean.

12. Leave to cool completely. Do not be tempted to tip the cake from the Bundt pan early—it will crumble!

13. While you are patiently waiting for the cake to cool, you can make your glaze. Mix the powdered sugar with buttermilk and fresh lemon juice by hand in a small bowl until the consistency is smooth. Once that sponge is completely cool, you can spoon, or delicately drizzle, the glaze so that it runs along the peaks of the sponge. The more abstract your glaze looks, the better, in my humble opinion. Not to mention that my decoration won Elspeth over too!

**Vampire Book Club: A Paranormal Women's Fiction Cozy
Mystery**

The Vampire Book Club - Book 1

Chapter and Curse - Book 2

A Spelling Mistake - Book 3

Vampire Knitting Club: Paranormal Cozy Mystery

Tangles and Treasons - a free prequel for Nancy's newsletter
subscribers

The Vampire Knitting Club - Book 1

Stitches and Witches - Book 2

Crochet and Cauldrons - Book 3

Stockings and Spells - Book 4

Purls and Potions - Book 5

Fair Isle and Fortunes - Book 6

Lace and Lies - Book 7

Bobbles and Broomsticks - Book 8

Popcorn and Poltergeists - Book 9

Garters and Gargoyles - Book 10

Diamonds and Daggers - Book 11

Cat's Paws and Curses a Holiday Whodunnit

The Great Witches Baking Show

The Great Witches Baking Show - Book 1

Baker's Coven - Book 2

A Rolling Scone - Book 3

A Bundt Instrument - Book 4

Blood, Sweat and Tiers - Book 5

Abigail Dixon 1920s Mysteries

Death of a Flapper - Book 1

Toni Diamond Mysteries

Toni is a successful saleswoman for Lady Bianca Cosmetics in this series of humorous cozy mysteries. Along with having an eye for beauty and a head for business, Toni's got a nose for trouble and she's never shy about following her instincts, even when they lead to murder.

Frosted Shadow - Book 1

Ultimate Concealer - Book 2

Midnight Shimmer - Book 3

A Diamond Choker For Christmas - A Toni Diamond Mysteries Novella

The Almost Wives Club

An enchanted wedding dress is a matchmaker in this series of romantic comedies where five runaway brides find out who the best men really are!

The Almost Wives Club: Kate - Book 1

Second Hand Bride - Book 2

Bridesmaid for Hire - Book 3

The Wedding Flight - Book 4

If the Dress Fits - Book 5

Take a Chance series

Meet the Chance family, a cobbled together family of eleven kids who are all grown up and finding their ways in life and love.

Kiss a Girl in the Rain - Book 1

Iris in Bloom - Book 2

Blueprint for a Kiss - Book 3

Every Rose - Book 4

Love to Go - Book 5

The Sheriff's Sweet Surrender - Book 6

The Daisy Game - Book 7

Chance Encounter - Prequel

Take a Chance Box Set - Prequel and Books 1-3

For a complete list of books, check out Nancy's website at
nancywarren.net

ABOUT THE AUTHOR

Nancy Warren is the USA Today Bestselling author of more than 90 novels. She's originally from Vancouver, Canada, though she tends to wander and has lived in England, Italy and California at various times. While living in Oxford she dreamed up The Vampire Knitting Club. She currently splits her time between Bath, UK, where she often pretends she's Jane Austen. Or at least a character in a Jane Austen novel, and Victoria, British Columbia where she enjoys living by the ocean. Favorite moments include being the answer to a cross-word puzzle clue in Canada's National Post newspaper, being featured on the front page of the New York Times when her book Speed Dating launched Harlequin's NASCAR series, and being nominated three times for Romance Writers of America's RITA award. She has an MA in Creative Writing from Bath Spa University. She's an avid hiker, loves chocolate and most of all, loves to hear from readers! The best way to stay in touch is to sign up for Nancy's newsletter at www.nancywarren.net or www.facebook.com/groups/NancyWarrenKnitwits

To learn more about Nancy and her books
www.nancywarren.net